HATCHET MAN

HATCHET MAN

PETER MOIR FOTHERINGHAM

ROBERT HALE · LONDON

ISBN 0 7090 5480 7

Robert Hale Limited
Clerkenwell House
Clerkenwell Green
London EC1R 0HT

Photoset in North Wales by
Derek Doyle & Associates, Mold, Clwyd.
Printed in Great Britain by
St Edmundsbury Press Ltd, Bury St Edmunds, Suffolk.
Bound by WBC Ltd, Bridgend, Mid-Glamorgan.

For Ian Philip, Jack Gemmell and Don Colamartino,
experts with the cold water treatment.
And for Alec Brown, who always had a better idea.

· **One** ·

John Greeve had been lying in a hole in the ground on a Swiss hillside for five days and nights with nothing but a sniper rifle for company and the strain was getting to him.

He had a camping mat under him; he lay in a four-seasons sleeping-bag inside a waterproof cover; he had food and water for two weeks and polythene bags to contain his body waste and keep the smell to an unobtrusive minimum; he had a selection of proprietary brands of indigestion tablets and anti-diarrhoea capsules and stimulants. But he was cold and damp and it was difficult to stop thinking back to the Lucerne hotel room he had left the week before, with its crisp sheets and spotless bathroom and delicious food.

He had brought nothing to read because he had known it would be dark in the hole and because he didn't want to be distracted from the job of watching the large villa 433 metres away on the far side of the lake and anyway he'd always been able to live at peace with his thoughts for long periods. But five days and nights in a hole in the ground was pushing it.

There was the dirt, the grit in the eyes and ears and between the teeth, the sticky crotch and armpits, the itching scalp and beard, the little things squirming and scurrying in the disturbed black soil and trying to join him inside the bag.

There was the persistent smell and clamminess of damp and dead vegetation.

All this was bad enough but what had really started bugging him towards the end of the third day was the way he couldn't stretch his arms or legs. The mental image he kept getting was of a coffin, with him in it, cramped and immobile. He should have dug a bigger hole, but he'd had just the hours of darkness of one summer night to do it and also make the two extra journeys over the ridge to bring in the stores, and he'd had to compromise. He'd had to carry the excavated soil well up the hill before dumping it and then he'd had to brush the area round the hole to obliterate the signs of his being there, and he had finished the job soaked in sweat just as the sky began to lighten. The five days since then had allowed the grass to recover.

He put his nose and mouth closer to the tiny grass-fringed opening and sucked cool fresh air into his lungs and worked hard at convincing himself he was cosy and safe and that it was good to be in a small hole in the ground and that the soil wasn't really going to collapse silently in all around him in the darkness and that the tree roots and nylon mesh holding up the turf roof wouldn't give way and that he wasn't really going to be suddenly buried and slowly suffocated.

It was early evening and the August sun was sitting on top of one of the mountains visible beyond the mouth of the valley. Another boring, glorious sunset.

Where the hell was Playboy?

The name Playboy had been a journalist's invention but it had stuck, partly because no one knew his real name and partly because of his rumoured reputation for enjoying the high life, the young women and good food, the fast cars and expensive hotels and probably the drugs.

But Playboy was a particularly inappropriate name. It should have been Terminator or Destroyer or Widowmaker, something like that, for he was believed to be personally responsible for the deaths of almost 400 people and the ghastly maiming and disfigurement of hundreds more. He was a terrorist, on hire to anyone prepared to pay the very high price he demanded for his services. He had been blamed for atrocities in Italy, Israel, France, England, South Africa; there was circumstantial evidence that another score of bombings and shootings might also be his responsibility; there were persistent stories that he ran a training camp somewhere in North Africa, where he and his men provided expert – and lucrative – instruction in the best and latest techniques for creating urban terror.

But if Playboy's notoriously ruthless security broke down and he were arrested it was unlikely that any court would find him guilty. There simply wasn't enough hard evidence and, if it came to the crunch, he would be able to call in old debts and influential people would provide unbreakable alibis. No one had ever come forward to grass on him. It was accepted that Playboy was inviolate.

Besides, even if he could be identified and located, no country would be willing to take on the responsibility of arresting him and holding him in prison. The people who worked with him would react by kidnapping a conference of VIPs or a busload of children and demand his release and he would walk free. And, when he was out of reach, there would be an explosion somewhere, in a main-line railway station or an airport or in a 747 at 35,000 feet, as punishment and to show other countries what to expect if they made the same mistake.

Something had to be done. He had to be killed.

John Greeve had been given the job.

*   *   *

Greeve's first kill – not counting military action – was back in 1981 when he was a sergeant with a certain regiment operating covertly in Northern Ireland. The man he killed was a 26-year-old IRA member who had been a terrorist since his early teens but whom no one had ever been able to catch. Maybe the man got cocky, maybe it was the drink, maybe it was just the Paddy factor. He stopped the stolen car he was driving just twenty metres from where Greeve was lying in the darkness at the side of a country road watching a deserted farmhouse for signs of activity. Greeve recognized him when the interior light came on as he opened the door and got out, unzipping his flies, and shot him twice in the chest with the silenced automatic pistol, walked back to the pick-up point and reported what he had done. The lieutenant swore and passed him on to the major. Greeve put his weapons on the desk and stood to attention, not caring much what happened.

'Why, Sergeant?'

'For Harper and Evans, sir.'

'They were my friends, too, but there are rules. Official policy.'

'Past caring, sir.'

'We're all tired. Tired and sick of it. I take it you're not planning a runner?'

'No, sir.'

'Consider youself confined to barracks till I get this bloody matter sorted out. It will probably be very bad for you but, off the record, I suspect I'd have done the same myself.'

Greeve was flown back to England the next day and kept locked up in a big house near Maidenhead for a week. On the Sunday afternoon he was taken down to a room full of worn furniture and threadbare carpets.

The man in the armchair beside the empty fireplace was small and elegant and fair-haired. He had one of those fine-skinned faces which make it difficult to estimate age, but Greeve made him maybe ten years older than himself. Greeve had never liked those shirts with the collars and cuffs white while the rest is striped; he'd never liked double-breasted suits; he'd never liked gold signet rings on a man, or expensive watches worn as jewellery, or silk handkerchiefs hanging from top pockets. He'd never liked smoothies. This man was everything he'd never liked. In the dozen years since he had not changed his opinion.

'Sit down, please, Sergeant. My name is Heward.'

The man fussed over the coffee, using sweeteners while Greeve spooned the brown sugar. This was the first man the sergeant had ever seen with manicured nails. He didn't like that either. At that time of John Greeve's life it would have been hard to find anything he did like.

'Please help yourself to a biscuit, Sergeant.'

Greeve didn't, on principle, although he wasn't sure what principle. He watched. While they talked Heward ate two digestive biscuits and not one single crumb landed on the immaculately pressed suit. People like that must get special training, he decided; probably at the school where they learn their accents. At that time he still had his broad regional twang; it was only later that he chose to eradicate it and adopt an anonymous middle-class BBC version.

'Your killing of that man has raised rather less of a furore than we'd expected, Sergeant. So many people hated him – or were frightened of him – that no one seems very sure just who might have been responsible. The security forces have been accused, of course; they always are. A denial was issued. The public will accept it; the IRA will have their doubts but will claim to know the truth.

Hopefully, the whole thing will blow over.'

'Does that mean I can go back to work?'

'I'd like to ask you some questions.'

'Ask away.' Greeve had the feeling he should be calling this man sir but he didn't feel like it.

'Why did you kill him?'

'He was a nasty.'

'Go on.'

'He killed people. He killed my friends.'

'You recognized him?'

'Immediately.'

'Did you hesitate?'

'What?'

'You recognized him. What went through your mind?'

'Not much.'

'How long between recognition and execution? Precisely.'

Greeve visualized the moment, counting. 'Three seconds.'

'You saw him, identified him, made a decision, raised your gun, aimed and fired twice.'

'Yes.'

'Did you check that he was dead?'

'Of course. Though there was no need.'

'I suppose not. Two heavy-calibre bullets in the centre of the chest are fairly conclusive. How did you feel afterwards?'

'Feel?'

'Oh, come on, Sergeant! I know you're not as thick as you're making out.' There was a cutting edge of authority now in Heward's voice. 'Did you feel guilt? Remorse? Doubt?'

'No.'

'Would you do it again?'

'Yes.'

'I mean, could you kill another man? A different man?'

'Not sure I follow you.'

'You know perfectly well what I mean.'

Greeve thought about it for a while. 'He was my first. I had good reason. So it was easy.'

Heward took a long cigarette from a gold case and lit it with a gold lighter. He held the cigarette like a woman. Greeve wondered if he might be a woofter but decided he wasn't.

'He wasn't your first, Sergeant.'

'He was my first like that.'

'So you need a good reason.'

'Of course.'

'How exactly did you feel afterwards? In the half-hour or so afterwards. While you were walking back to the pick-up. How did you react?'

'Cold. Fatalistic. Unrepentant.'

'You could have gone to university. Why didn't you?'

The sudden change of tack made Greeve pause for a moment. 'Money. Or the lack of it.'

'You come from a broken family.'

'Yes.'

'Do you keep in touch?'

'No.'

'Have you any idea who I am?'

'I'd make a guess at MI5.'

'Wrong. Did you have any plans for when you left the Army?'

Greeve noted the use of the past tense. 'Hadn't thought that far ahead.'

'Time you did. I'm offering you a job.'

'I have one.'

'No.'

You don't usually get out of the Army that easily, Greeve thought sourly.

'Tell me about the job.'

'Sometimes we need people excised.'

'Excised?'

'The current euphemism. There's always a very good reason why we need it done, and an equally good reason why we can't rely on the slow wheels of justice.'

'Not interested.'

'The people I'm talking about are people like your man in Armagh, except that they're scattered all over the world. Sometimes it has to be done that way, which means someone has to take on the job. Someone has to accept the responsibility. It's not something we do lightly. There's a retainer and a premium.'

'What does that mean?'

'£25,000 a year plus £5,000 on successful completion of a contract, plus all reasonable expenses. In cash, tax-free. Your pension is something you'd have to take care of yourself, because there can be no traceable link between you and us. There's a car every two years, which you would buy and for which you would be reimbursed in cash on production of the necessary receipt. To a limit of £7,000: if you wanted to swan around in a Jag or whatever, you'd have to pay the difference yourself.'

This was in 1981. It was very good money, and it had risen steadily since then.

'So I'd be working for MI6?' It seemed the obvious alternative.

'You would have no connection at all with anyone. If the crunch came no one would admit to any knowledge of you. I would deny ever having met you and if you persisted I would produce evidence that you had a record of pretending to be an employee of the Secret Intelligence Service. It's been done before.'

'But I'd still be working for MI6.'

'You would be working for me. Leave it at that.'

'How many jobs a year?'

'Maybe one, maybe two. We're not talking mass executions.'

Greeve didn't give much for his chances on the labour market. His qualifications were hardly the kind to make an interesting c.v. and he didn't fancy driving a delivery van or stacking supermarket shelves. Maybe if he did it for a couple of years and saved hard he'd be able to get out and start a small business somewhere, selling fishing tackle and guns. Or maybe he was being naive.

'Let me think about it.'

'I'd like an answer by the end of the week. Just let Mr Cogger know you want to speak to me.'

That was on the Sunday. Greeve thought about it until the Wednesday but he'd made up his mind long before then.

433 metres away the French window at the back of the villa opened and the swarthy man with the moustache came out and the two dogs followed, as they had done several times every day since Greeve arrived. The dogs were Dobermans, beautiful creatures. Greeve had always had a special feeling for anything constructed to do a job efficiently, with no frills, no ornament: a Beretta 92F, a Stanley plane, a Parker 61 fountain pen, a Land Rover, a working dog.

There was no barking, no prancing around. The dogs separated, taking one side of the house each. They checked out the big garden, not wasting their time on interesting smells, not pausing to lift a leg until they were satisfied that their patch was clear of intruders. The swarthy man followed. He didn't need the knee-length leather coat on this mild evening but it served to hide the Uzi or whatever he was carrying.

The valley was silent. The road at the far side of the villa

continued for another mile or so and ended at a disused
barn. The big house was isolated, almost a mile from the
nearest dwellings downhill. The garden sloped down to a
jetty at the side of the lake. Greeve's hole in the ground
was directly opposite, on the other side of the mirror-like
water, about a hundred metres into the trees and twenty
metres higher than the terrace. He had a clear view over
the tops of the lower trees to the back of the house.

He watched the man with the dogs through the
Schmidt and Bender telescopic sight on the Walther
WA2000. He was in his hole in the ground because this
man had rented another house in Switzerland for the
month of August the previous year and there was
tenuous evidence that Playboy had spent two weeks in
that house. This man had been under intermittent
surveillance ever since. He had rented the villa and
moved in a week back.

Greeve was lying in the hole in the faint hope that
Playboy would appear and that he would be able to excise
him.

There was no urgency about the way the swarthy man
patrolled the garden, nothing to suggest he was expecting
Playboy to arrive in the immediate future.

Maybe the whole thing was a non-starter.

Greeve lowered the rifle and watched him stroll out to
the end of the wooden jetty and rock the moored rowing
boat with his foot. Ripples spread across the smooth
water, destroying the reflection of the villa. One of the
Dobermans pissed against a tree. The man turned and
walked slowly back up the path to the house and sat on
an ornamental wrought-iron bench and lit a cigarette. The
dogs, relaxed, were sniffing around and pawing at
interesting bits of garden.

Greeve had pretty well given up smoking, but he wanted
one now. He'd been wanting one for the past five days.

* * *

It was late on the seventh day when a Mercedes estate came up the road fast and swung into the driveway leading to the house. It rocked to a stop half-hidden beyond the double garage and four men got out. Greeve watched through the 'scope, comparing the faces with the grainy enlargement of the black and white passport photograph he had studied for hours on end back in London, ready to shoot if he identified Playboy and had the chance of a definite kill.

Something about the way the four men moved told him Playboy was not among them. None of these men was being protected by the others. They were soldiers, armed but keeping their weapons hidden, alert, suspicious.

The dogs appeared from a side door he couldn't see, dragging their man, barking. There was a pause of a minute or two while he reassured them and introduced the new arrivals. Then there was a brief conversation, cases were unloaded and carried inside, one of the new arrivals taken on a tour of the garden.

Greeve began to be cautiously optimistic.

They were all dark-faced, Middle-Eastern in origin, black-haired. He watched their leader as he walked out along the jetty and studied the trees across the lake. He looked a lot like the face in the photograph; perhaps the rumours about Playboy having a brother as second-in-command were based on fact. Whoever he was, he clearly had authority. He was also a snappy dresser. Greeve was no expert, but the tan lightweight suit had the smell of money about it. The others were more the leather-jacket-and-sweatshirt types.

They all vanished inside the house and Greeve tried to interpret everything he had seen.

The first man, the one with the dogs, had rented the

house and taken entry. Two weeks later, tonight, an
advance party had arrived. They would check the place
out, search it for bugs, move out into the surrounding
countryside looking for problems. They would already
have information on everyone living in the expensive
houses further down the valley. If everything was safe
Playboy would receive a signal and come in.

Maybe.

Maybe what Greeve was seeing was an Egyptian pop
group or a Lebanese film crew or a Libyan investment
team.

But he didn't think so.

He didn't see any of them again until the following
morning. By that time they must have checked out the
house from top to bottom and failed to find anything
suspicious. They wouldn't. It was standard practice that
the official investigators stayed well away from Greeve's
targets. He was given what details were available of
where and when he might find his latest contract and
then everyone cleared the area. No bugs, no surveillance,
no painfully innocent men washing windows or claiming
to be engineers come to fix the telephone. This wasn't a
TV movie. Playboy and his soldiers were paranoid about
security. One hint of anything suspicious and they would
vanish like frost on a hot day.

They all left the house about ten in the morning,
splitting up to walk slowly and very casually over the
surrounding countryside, eyes to the ground, stopping
frequently to study anything that caught their attention.
Greeve didn't like the way the leader kept looking over to
this side of the lake and the way he used binoculars to
scan the hillside. He felt the temptation to move his head
back from the tiny hole in the grass when the big lenses
seemed to settle right on him.

The man looked right and left and Greeve knew what

he was thinking. The narrow lake ran almost half a mile in each direction from the jetty, never more than about 300 metres wide. He wanted to come over and search the ground on this side. He spoke into a radio and two of the soldiers joined him on the jetty; they climbed into the dinghy and started rowing across.

It would have been easy to blow them away when they were half-way across, but they weren't the target. All Greeve could do was strip the protective polythene off the rifle, check the Beretta pistol and wait to see what happened.

He didn't like the way they were coming straight towards him.

· **Two** ·

Heward's guess that there might be one or perhaps two contracts a year had been way out. In twelve years Greeve had excised just nine men and one woman.

He was told only what he needed to know about the targets. Names, sometimes, although that wasn't always necessary; addresses or locations, of course; photographs or videos, usually; habits, patterns, personal quirks, car numbers, anything which might help to ensure a clean kill. The one thing he always insisted on was knowing why. He needed a motive. He had to have a good reason for killing someone.

But now three armed men were trying to beach a small boat among the reeds and water plants a hundred yards downhill from his hole in the ground and if they found him he would have to kill in self-defence and that would be failure. Playboy would vanish back to wherever he normally hid out and the chance would be lost and he would carry on working and innocent people would die. Greeve didn't like the idea. It would be difficult to live with the consequences of that kind of failure. If he survived.

The boat was just visible through the branches of the trees along the water's edge. It seemed to have become jammed among the reeds. He could hear the men arguing, then the leader snapped an order and one of them stepped out and sank thigh-deep into the soft mud below the surface, his other leg stuck up at a ludicrous angle against the gunnel. He tried to recover and the dinghy rocked wildly. He was left standing up to his waist in the lake, holding on to the boat, cursing furiously while the other two stared at him with grins on their dark faces. He couldn't see the joke.

He tried to struggle ashore but the mud was too deep so they hauled him in over the transom and rowed back towards the jetty. The leader's gestures made it clear that they would have to search Greeve's side of the valley by walking down to the wooden footbridge crossing the stream which ran out of the tail of the lake and then making their way back up the shore. It was clear that he took his duties seriously.

Greeve ate a small meal, went through the distasteful business of emptying his bowels into a polythene bag, washed himself with a handful of moist tissues, checked out the guns yet again and decided he was as ready as he could be for fight or flight. By that time he could hear the search party coming up the near side of the lake. He had watched them leave the house and there were four of them now, the man with the dogs replacing the one who had tried to wade ashore. Greeve didn't like the idea of the dogs sniffing around. The men might not see his hole in the ground but the dogs would get his scent: it was now seven days since he'd last been within shouting distance of soap and water.

They were working their way along the shore, slowly, about ten feet apart, their murmuring voices carrying in the windless air. He made plans. The leader first, then the two other soldiers in turn; the man with the dogs last; then the dogs. If he got the chance. Then the ignominious retreat up the hillside and over the ridge and down to where he had buried a polythene bag containing a set of hillwalker's clothes and a rucksack. Then down to the main road and into the nearest village and away, to contact Heward and explain that the whole year's work had been wasted and they'd have to start again. Which wouldn't go down at all well.

They passed below him and kept going until they vanished from sight. Half an hour later they came back, the search pattern moved to a thirty-foot wide swathe further uphill. By mid-afternoon they were within what seemed like spitting distance and he could see their faces clearly and hear what they were saying even if he couldn't understand the language. They were tired and hot and probably hungry and their flash shoes weren't standing up to the rough ground too well but there was no sign that they were becoming careless. The dogs were still on the leads, tireless and eager. When they reached the end of this sweep and turned and came back the hole in the ground would be right in the middle of their area of search.

He let them get almost out of sight then moved the safety catch on the rifle.

He saw them stop. The leader was using the walkie-talkie. Across the lake the remaining member of the party was standing on the terrace speaking into the handset. Greeve looked back through the trees in time to see the leader nodding, putting his set back in his pocket, making a gesture with one hand.

They all walked away with that slight change in body language which means, the job's finished, let's take a break. Across the lake, the other man was standing in the open French window speaking into a telephone.

Playboy was coming. Greeve was sure of it.

He had always been good with a gun, despite never

having had anything more than a borrowed .177 air pistol
in his hands before he left the acrimonious disorder of the
back-to-back house for the cheerful discipline of army life.
From the very start he found the various firearms things
of pleasure. He loved the precise, no-nonsense *purpose-
fulness* of them. He loved the shape and the feel and the
weight and the gleam of precisely milled metal. He loved
the power of them; loved the way he could sight on to a
tiny target a long way off and squeeze the trigger and
send a bullet spinning through the air to hit that point.
His talent was recognized and he was given extra
training. Later he was allowed to try for that other
regiment and made the grade and his training was
extended to include other weapons, other ways of killing.
He loved it. He'd found his purpose in life. He'd found
some self-respect.

   He went home just once, about six months after joining
up. The man in the vest and pyjama trousers who opened
the door was neither his violent father nor the man his
mother had been living with when he left. He had to
explain who he was before the man let him in. His mother
came downstairs pulling on a robe, her greasy hair
hanging over her face. Greeve said he'd just popped in to
say hello and that he couldn't stop; he didn't even sit
down. He left and took the train back to camp and never
returned, never wrote, never even sent a Christmas card.
After that, the Army was where he lived. Since leaving the
Army to work for Heward he had never had anywhere
that might be called a home of his own. He travelled light,
one small suitcase and a flight bag.

It was almost an hour before anything much happened
across the lake. Greeve sensed something was due to
happen when all five of them and the dogs appeared and
they wandered about in that overly innocent way of all

men who carry weapons and have the job of ensuring someone's safety. He had done it himself: no matter how hard you try to appear unobtrusive and casual, you always look like some kind of gunslinger. The body just doesn't look natural.

He heard the car engine at the same time as the men around the villa heard it. A deep, throaty roar. He knew then, when he heard the engine, that Playboy's life was approaching its end.

The low red shape came up the road much too fast and swung into the drive and stopped dead. Greeve didn't need to see the single rear-view mirror to recognize it as a Ferrari Testarossa. The soldiers clustered around, making the car look like it was two feet high.

Greeve used the 'scope to follow the figure who climbed out but there was no chance of a clear shot. It was Playboy, all right. The passport photograph came to life in the fleshy dark face. He was even wearing the same kind of moustache. Suede blouson jacket, pale-blue shirt, faded denims, suede chukka boots. Gold at the throat and both wrists and on several fingers. Big yellow smile. The clear indications of a spreading gut. He was hustled inside then his cases were taken in and that was the last Greeve saw of him that night.

The eighth day was wet. The rain trickled steadily into the hole in the ground and Greeve could hear little landslides of soft wet earth and feel the weight of the soil against his legs and tried not to get worried.

Nothing showed across the lake until midday, when two of the soldiers left in the Mercedes, to return late in the afternoon with three young women. They all went inside. The sound of rock music came faintly across the water. Darkness fell. The party went on for a long time. The Mercedes left again at ten the following morning, taking the women back to wherever they'd come from and, too quickly for Greeve to do anything about it, Playboy appeared, his body hidden by his brother and the other minder, to get into the Ferrari and drive off in a roar of engine noise and a spray of gravel.

He returned in mid-afternoon.

Greeve heard the sound of the Ferrari and fitted the earplugs to protect himself from the concussion of the rifle.

Maybe Playboy had eaten too big a lunch. Maybe he'd drunk too much. Maybe he was just shagged out after the night before. Whatever it was, he was careless. He paused for one vital moment when he climbed out of the car, tucking his shirt into his trousers, pulling in the softening belly.

Greeve's first shot killed him. The second was insurance. The third was just in case. Playboy collapsed backwards across the Ferrari, his blood mottling the glass of the windscreen, then slid to the ground in a properly graceless position. Greeve had time to reload. The WH2000 is an incredible machine but the magazine holds just six rounds and there were still three armed men over there and it was bright daylight and he had to get away. He waited.

Two men came out of the house, running, one to throw himself protectively but uselessly over the body, the other, the brother, to cover as many points of the compass as he could. The brother had an Uzi and the soldier was carrying an Ingram Model 10. Greeve waited until he had a clear sight on Playboy's brother and took him out with a sweet shot through the head.

The WH2000 is ideal for anyone operating from a cramped hole in the ground. It's a sniper rifle but without the usual disadvantage of a long barrel; instead, it is cleverly constructed so that the end of the barrel is on top of the butt, close to the shoulder, which allowed him to keep the business end inside the hole. The crack of the shots was muffled and the valley created confusing echoes and the remaining man on the far side of the lake had no idea where the shots were coming from. Greeve had cut right down on the oil and was shooting from inside a hole so there was no blue smoke to give him away but his precautions were hardly necessary. He was able to excise the last man before there was any returning fire. The man with the dogs didn't appear.

Greeve dropped the rifle but kept the pistol and slid out of the sleeping-bag and up through the hole into the open and rolled into cover behind a tree. Nothing happened. 433 metres away the dogs bounded out of the house, barking their warnings, and the last man followed. He was more interested in finding cover than anything else and Greeve slipped away through the trees, heading uphill.

The climb was difficult after the nine days in the hole in the ground. It felt as if the muscles in his legs had atrophied and his lungs had shrunk. After a few hundred feet on the steep climb he had to stop and lean against a tree, gasping for breath. After that he took it more gently, pacing himself, controlling his breathing. It took about an hour to reach the top of the ridge and then it wasn't too bad. An hour after that he managed to find the bag he had hidden and made the change, substituting a colourful shirt and jersey and breeches and long red stockings for the camouflage suit. He buried everything he didn't need, hid the automatic pistol separately, then pulled on the rucksack and walked down the track into the village, stopping to wash his face and hands in a stream on the way. Half an hour later he was dozing in the back seat of a bus.

*　*　*

He kept going, using a succession of local buses, until he reached a village just before dark. He checked in at a small hotel where they didn't seem at all surprised at his appearance and went up to his room. This was what he'd been promising himself for nine days. He shaved carefully and trimmed his nails and stood under the shower for half an hour, shampooing his hair four times, scrubbing every inch of his body with soap and flannel. Then he dressed, went out and ate a hot meal and drank a bottle of red wine and smoked two cigarettes.

If anyone managed to discover the hole in the ground they would find nothing to identify him. There were no fingerprints on anything, because he'd been wearing the thin leather gloves for the whole nine days. The rifle was German, supplied by Heward, its provenance obscured; the food and the bottles of water had been purchased in several supermarkets in Lucerne; the sleeping-bag was Swiss Army surplus. Analysing the bags of crap and piss would tell them nothing. He had arrived in darkness and left as one of the thousands of walkers and climbers who clutter the Swiss Alps during the summer.

Besides, it was unlikely that the man with the dogs was going to call the police.

Greeve left Switzerland the following morning still dressed as a walker and arrived in Dijon early in the afternoon looking like a tourist. He chose a hotel in the middle of the town, checked in, went back out for some food then used a public phone in a café.

'Yes?'

'My name's Paddy Peutherer. Mr Lomax, please.'

'I'm afraid you have a wrong number.'

'I'll wait until Christmas.'

'You have a wrong number.'

'I'm calling in.'

'One moment.'

Heward came on at once. 'Yes, Sergeant?'

'I've tied up that contract. Our man's brother and one other came with the deal.'

'Definitely signed up?'

'Definitely.'

'Well done, Sergeant. Your commission will be paid next time we meet. Keep in touch.'

'Anything happening at the moment?'

'No, nothing. But you should read the current edition of *Time* magazine. An article by Lisa Castelle.'

Greeve bought a copy of *Time* at a newsstand and read it over coffee and cognac in the cool depths of a bistro. Lisa Castelle wrote that she did not accept that her father had been involved in the drugs trade. He had been a liberal but he had been American through and through and a fine man and a great writer and a good father. He played around and was divorced and drank too much, but he was a man of vision and commitment and he had been murdered to keep him quiet. He had been investigating a high-level gun-running operation and he had been getting too near the truth, she said. The evidence pointing to his being killed as the result of some squalid argument about drugs had been faked. She was sure of it and she was going to prove it.

She was on the right track. Greeve had killed Hugo Castelle twelve months before, in a hotel room in Marseille, using a Walther P5 wrapped in a towel. He had planted the drugs and left the gun behind knowing that a ballistics check would identify it as the weapon which had been used in the murder of a pusher in the same town six months earlier.

He wondered if Lisa Castelle really believed what she

wrote, or if she knew her father had been an Iraqi recruit ever since the two years he spent in Baghdad as Iraq correspondent for a New York magazine. Maybe she knew but had to clear the air for herself. It didn't matter much.

There was a picture of Lisa Castelle. She had the kind of face that grabs a man and makes him wish he were special enough to attract the attention of a woman like that. Straight black hair worn shoulder-length and expertly cut; big dark eyes; narrow nose; full mouth, beautifully modelled. A hint, in her face and her name, of some kind of Latin ancestry. The parts were conventional, but on her everything added up to a most unusual whole.

Greeve studied the picture for a long time then read the article again. A box alongside gave the information that Lisa Castelle was a writer, like her father, with one successful non-fiction book and a number of short stories to her credit. Greeve had read the book and remembered it. She had told the stories of half-a-dozen Vietnam veterans and how they coped with the stress and trauma of that terrible war. It had been well written, well researched, compassionate and thoughtful. He remembered being surprised that she had managed to get close enough to these shattered and suspicious men to get their confidence and their stories. The book had won a prestigious award in the States.

She was twenty-seven, a graduate of UCLA, a successful magazine writer before she wrote her bestselling book. She had been devoted to her father and had learned much of her writing from him.

Why had Heward brought this to his attention? Greeve hated having his targets come alive after he'd killed them. He didn't want to read about their families, their wives and children, their fondness for pets, their good works, their interest in fly fishing or chess or Mozart. Perhaps this was why he preferred to kill from a distance: it separated him from the target, made the target anonymous, denied the target a personality.

Lisa Castelle was an experienced researcher and journalist and she undoubtedly had charm. Everything indicated she was determined and committed: she would unearth whatever there was to be learned about the death of her father. Greeve was unworried by the possibility. There was no connection between him and Hugo Castelle. The evidence he had planted was sound and he had left no trail. She would be up against a brick wall.

But it would have been good to meet her and maybe get to know her.

He bought a change of clothes, had his hair cut, went back to the hotel, showered and changed and went out for a meal. He sat alone, trying not to feel conspicuous among the crowded tables.

Afterwards he hailed a taxi and asked the driver about where to find a woman.

The two short streets were busy with prostitutes and he took his time making up his mind what he wanted. His final choice was perhaps eighteen years old and looked like the young Brigitte Bardot, or thought she did. She had used cheap scent to disguise the fact that the sheets were dirty and, without the support of a bra, her breasts sagged loosely. He left in a bad mood, annoyed that what should have been a pleasant release after the nine days of strain had turned out to be so unsatisfactory.

Walking back to the hotel, seeing the couples in the streets and cafés, he felt the old sense of loss coming back and, for once, did nothing to suppress the emotion.

Where was Gilly now? He'd had no contact with her since that day eleven years before when everything had come to an explosive head. She had tried to understand and cope with his long absences, his tension, his

occasional nightmares, his long weeks of doing nothing
but read books and go to museums and art galleries; she
had pretended to accept his story of having a private
income and being an amateur art dealer; but there had
been so little proof and so many inconsistencies that her
suspicions had grown like a fungus until even her gentle
and loving nature could take no more.

The contract in Lagos had lasted three weeks instead of
the two days he had anticipated and the kill had been
difficult and dangerous and messy. When he returned to
London he was exhausted and on a razor's edge and her
tears and accusations had been the last straw. The row
continued over most of an evening and then he walked
out, knowing it was the only thing he could do for
someone he loved, knowing he should never have
allowed the affair to start in the first place, knowing he
had been selfish in wanting a loving relationship with a
woman when he killed for a living.

But he still missed her. He missed loving and being
loved. He missed the intimacy and the gentleness and the
caring and the laughter and the plans for the future.

He had no idea how many women he had used over the
years since then. A few were memorable, at least for a
while, but the rest were faceless and forgotten. No matter
how many and how often, they were little more than
assisted masturbation, and there were times when the
need for a woman, rather than the need for physical relief,
became almost more than he could bear.

He wondered what Lisa Castelle was like in bed.

· Three ·

The man Greeve knew as Heward waited while the Director's secretary used the intercom.

'Mr Lacey, sir.... Thank you.' She released the switch and gave Lacey a smile that lacked warmth; she had never liked the little man with the receding fair hair and fussy manners. 'He'll see you now, Mr Lacey.'

'Thank you.'

Lacey passed through the heavy door and closed it carefully behind him. The Director sat square and rather daunting behind the massive desk, his thick white hair glowing in the light of the standard lamp behind his left shoulder. The curtains were drawn; they were always drawn, night and day.

'Sit down, Lacey. Good news, I hope. I've had a bellyful of bad news today.'

He overdoes the bluff old soldier bit, Lacey thought. He was only a bloody major in Military Intelligence before he transferred to us.

'Yes, sir, good news. You'll recall I was instructed to take steps to excise the terrorist Playboy. I put my man on to it and he's called in to say he's been successful. He also excised a man who may have been Playboy's brother, as well as a bodyguard. It was always rumoured that Playboy's brother was his second-in-command.'

'I know. This is definite, is it?'

'I've never had any reason to think my man exaggerates, sir. He has never done so in the past.'

'Sounds a bit gung-ho. What the hell did he use?'

'We provided a sniper rifle, sir.'

The Director looked doubtful. 'Do you have confirmation?'

'Not yet, sir. We'll keep our ears open. It's unlikely to reach the media: I'd expect Playboy's staff to clear up the mess as unobtrusively as possible.'

'So your man could be lying?'

Lacey tried hard to contain his annoyance. Until he eased himself into the top job eighteen months back the Director had never heard of Greeve. He still didn't know the assassin's name, and never would. In the whole organization only Lacey had that information.

'My man has been working for us for twelve years, sir. He is totally reliable and completely honest. If he fails, he reports his failure. And he's failed only once.'

'All right, Lacey, all right. I'm not criticizing. But you will try to get confirmation.'

'Of course, sir.'

'I think you told me there's no chance of a link between us and whatshisname. No danger of anything blowing up in my face?'

'No chance, sir. I'm the only person who knows who he is, and he doesn't know who I am. He's not on the books and it would be impossible to trace his payments back to us.'

'Very well. I'll reserve my congratulations until we know for definite, but if Playboy's really dead I'd like your chap to know we're appreciative of his efforts.'

'I'll let him know, sir.'

'Good man. Anything else?'

'No, sir.' Lacey rose. 'Thank you, sir.'

A word of thanks to me wouldn't have gone amiss, he thought as he closed the door behind him. I mean, we only worked on this one for a whole bloody year.

The hotel on the northern fringe of Kensington hid its quality behind a very plain frontage. Lacey arrived a little before eight in the evening and went straight up to a suite on the third floor and was admitted by a very wide man with short hair and eyes like ice. This was Rossi, Eugene Carver's bodyguard. In six years Lacey had never heard Rossi speak more than an occasional word.

Carver was seated at a table while a waiter served from a trolley. Steam rose and there was the smell of meat.

'Sit down, Lacey. I ordered steak for you. OK?' The Texan voice was loud and confident.

Another massive steak. Carver, Lacey knew, quite often had steak and eggs for breakfast. With champagne. The idea sickened him. He sat down across the table from Carver and watched in dismay as the waiter laid a pound or so of bleeding meat in front of him.

'French fries, sir?'

'Just the salad.'

Carver never seemed to get any fatter, which made no sense. He was already huge, well over six feet tall and barrel-chested, but the waistline did not appear to have grown any larger in six years and the flesh under the blue chin was still firm. He had to be in his mid-fifties by now, but the only indication of deterioration was the way the hairpieces had gradually developed into a full wig. Oddly, Carver made no attempt to hide the fact that he wore a rug, changing abruptly from an *en brosse* style in dark brown to a longish affair in black shot with grey. He seemed to wear wigs as other men wore hats. The big square face was deeply tanned, the grey eyes sharp and penetrating, the nose suspiciously narrow, as if it had been altered surgically. He was a man who spent a lot of money on his clothes.

Lacey watched the huge hands sever a cube of steak; the fork was transferred to the right hand, the meat conveyed to the thick-lipped mouth; strong teeth made short work of reducing it to a pulp ready for swallowing. A mouthful of wine cleansed the palate. Lacey picked up his knife and fork reluctantly and took a little salad. The waiter left.

'He heard you use my name. That was careless.'

'I realized that as soon as I said it, my friend. My apologies. Try your steak. It's good.'

'I'm not really hungry.' Lacey forced himself to eat a small slice of the meat. The centre was red and wet. There was enough on his plate to make a steak pie for six people. 'What's the latest?'

'We're busy. Very busy.' Carver talked but without slowing his rate of intake. He had consumed his steak and was busy with Stilton and oatcakes before he finished speaking. 'Anything yet on the Castelle broad?'

'Yes. From a rather unexpected source. I've had word from a Belgian friend that Lisa Castelle has made contact with Bodo Roth and that they are to meet in Paris on Tuesday the 24th.'

'Bodo Roth? Christ, it's a long time since I heard that name. Who's the Belgian friend?'

'That's classified. Someone close to Roth. He's been on our payroll for several years.'

'So the information is hard?'

'Yes.'

'So that puts her in Paris on a certain day. Maybe we should grab the chance and wipe her.'

Lacey pushed his plate away. He had eaten only a small part of the steak.

'Is she really that dangerous?'

Carver took time out to gather a burp and release it loudly. 'She could become dangerous. She could learn something. Someone might talk. I don't need that kind of problem. I want her dead.'

Lacey could read the uncertainty in the American's voice. Carver just wasn't being as aggressive and decisive as usual.

'It's too soon to put a contract on her. My man is squeamish about killing women. He's done it just once before and it took me a long time to get him sufficiently motivated. It didn't go well and he was badly affected afterwards. I think he was almost tempted to give up the work.'

'So get someone else.'

'Running a hatchet man isn't quite like employing a bookkeeper or a secretary. They're very hard to find and they're expensive and if they're good they're worth their weight in gold. My man is very good. But one of the rules of the game is that he has the option of turning down a contract if he believes it to be beyond his capability or too dangerous. He hasn't turned one down yet, but he almost did with … with the woman I mentioned. It took me some time to motivate him. I anticipate the same difficulty with Lisa Castelle. She is, after all, young and very beautiful and altogether someone to be admired. It will be difficult to motivate my man sufficiently until he has already seen for himself that she is suspect.'

Carver appeared to be concentrating on igniting a green cigar, but Lacey knew better than to doubt his attention. Or his intelligence.

'So you get your man to scrub Bodo Roth while the broad is with him. Then your man thinks she's tied up with the creep.'

'Exactly. When he reports back he will mention her. I shall sound surprised but not too surprised. This appears to confirm our suspicions, I shall say. Lisa Castelle is tarred with the same brush as her father. Later, when I issue a contract on her, he will already be half-convinced.'

'Sounds good. Have a drink. Scotch?'

'Yes.'

The bodyguard moved to the bottles on the side table and poured. Lacey accepted his glass and sipped.

'You have something for me?'

'Sure thing.'

Carver took a long envelope from an inside pocket and tossed it over the table. Lacey caught it before it landed on the cooling steak and glanced inside. The money represented something over his annual salary and he received a similar sum every three months, with an occasional bonus. From what he earned from Carver he had to pay the premiums Greeve collected for unofficial kills, the ones the poor fool thought were sanctioned by the people Lacey worked for, and there were a few incidental expenses like hotel rooms and weapons, but the return on the investment was still immense.

How long would it go on? The longer the better, Lacey decided. Angela's only hobby was spending money and the school fees were ridiculous and they had both grown accustomed to a certain way of life. His rise in the office had not been as rapid as he had anticipated and there was a definite feeling, unspoken, that by his age he should have been further up the tree, which suggested he could not anticipate further promotion. The money was a very satisfactory compensation.

'Horny, my friend? Shall we send out for something juicy?'

Lacey looked over the table at the Texan's broad grin and nodded diffidently.

· Four ·

The routine was for Greeve to call Heward during a two-hour time-slot every Wednesday afternoon. He didn't know the name of the woman who answered the phone and she probably didn't know his real name, which he hadn't used in twelve years. They recognized each other's voice but always went through the parole: he would ask for Mr Lomax and give himself a name with alliterative capitals, she would say he had a wrong number and he would reply that he was prepared to wait some impracticable length of time. If there was nothing for him she would repeat that he had a wrong number and that would be the end of it. If he had a report to make he would say he was calling in.

If there was a contract Heward would come on and they would make arrangements to meet and when they did Heward would brief him and deliver whatever material was available. Greeve would study the material and watch the video if there was one and make notes and return all the paperwork. He was allowed to keep still photographs on the strict understanding that he destroyed them and the notes before going anywhere near the target. Greeve would make his plans and Heward would supply whatever weapons or equipment were required. Greeve never knew what position Heward

occupied in whatever organization they worked for, and
Heward was the only person in the organization who had
ever seen Greeve.

Greeve stayed in Dijon for three days of rest and
recuperation. The girl he chose on the second night was
overweight but amusing and clean and earned her money.

It was still August and France was unpleasantly hot and
he had never been a sun-worshipper so he caught a flight
out on the Saturday morning to find London muggy and
unpleasant. He checked the departure information screens
and, on an impulse, decided to fly to Orkney. He had been
there once before, not on business, and the place appealed
to him. He felt a strong desire to experience the refreshing
wind and the huge sky and the empty beaches, recognizing that this was probably a reaction to the nine days in
the hole in the ground in Switzerland.

He rented a Nova at Kirkwall airport and drove into the
town and a girl in the tourist office beside the cathedral
located a cancelled booking. He bought an Ordnance
Survey 1:50000 sheet and drove across Mainland and
found the house; the landlady must have been watching
for him because she walked down the track from the farm
as soon as he parked the car.

'Mr Davidson?'

'Yes. Hello. I take it you're Mrs Flett?'

'That's right. Come away in. You're lucky; we were
booked solid, but some policemen couldn't get up for the
fishing because they had to be in court. Is it just yourself?'

'Just me, yes.'

'You'll find it a bit big. You'd be better in the peerie
house, but it's taken.'

'I like room to move around. I'll pay you now.' That
meant he could leave any time he wanted, if necessary
without letting her know. It was a routine precaution.

The former farmhouse had beds enough to sleep six. It

was clean and comfortable and overlooked the long curve of sand and blue waters of Skaill Bay and the prehistoric village of Skara Brae. He bought sufficient food and alcohol to get through the weekend from a shop a couple of miles along the Birsay road and made macaroni and cheese and wholemeal toast and opened a bottle of wine.

There was a television set but he chose instead to look at the two books he had bought in London. They were both hardbacks, both expensive. The photograph on the dust jacket of one of them showed Lisa Castelle, this time with her black hair tightly curled in a pre-Raphaelite style which emphasized her graceful neck and made her look decidedly intellectual. She was very beautiful. The big dark eyes were staring straight into the camera, straight into his eyes, and he sat there for a long time memorizing that face the way he studied the photographs of his contracts, feature by feature, until he knew he would be able to recognize her instantly, from a distance, in any situation.

He had already been through this exercise less than a year back with the face on the other dust jacket. He had already killed Hugo Castelle. He remembered the thinning dark hair, overlong and untidy at the back, and the lean features, the slightly olive skin, the deep lines round the eyes and mouth. He remembered the smell of pipe tobacco and wondered if the pipe Hugo Castelle was smoking in the photograph was the one he had bitten through when the bullets hit. Greeve remembered the look of puzzlement when the writer realized there was an automatic pistol inside the towel.

'Why?'

That was the only word Greeve ever heard him say. He could have told him why but you must never communicate with the contract, never allow even the briefest human relationship to develop. It weakens you, raises doubts; it's so much easier to kill a stranger. Anyway, there's always the danger the target might start shouting or throwing himself about and then the whole thing becomes untidy. You don't produce the gun until it's time to do the killing and then you don't hesitate.

Greeve had read Lisa Castelle's book and would read it again but for the moment he was more interested in Hugo Castelle's version of the Irangate story. He checked the printing history and saw that the first edition had been published just three months before the American died; it seemed likely that this edition had been produced to capitalize on the publicity surrounding his death.

Greeve had always been a reader. There had been plenty of quiet time over the previous twelve years and he'd used it to educate himself. He had no friends, no acquaintances even, no home, no wife or lover; he didn't own a car because when he had one it restricted his movements and spent too much of its time clocking up huge bills in airport car-parks. He didn't miss any of these things, but he often wished he had a bookcase somewhere. He couldn't carry the books with him, not in any number, so he bought them and read them and threw them away and he didn't like doing that.

He read until about eleven then went out and walked down over the fields and along the beach. In the long northern twilight there was still light enough to see clearly. For once there was just the faintest of breezes and he savoured a silence broken only by the gentle slap of small waves on the sand and the occasional cry of a seabird.

It all made Hugo Castelle's claustrophobic story of secret deals and money laundering, hostages and drugs and arms seem remote and almost irrelevant. Castelle had been a good writer, his prose lively and lucid, and Greeve was impressed by the way he had refused to give up when the trail went cold and obstacles were put in his way. The book was an account of his investigations as well as the story of Irangate itself and that was what made it all so fascinating. It was almost a thriller.

Castelle had been a brave man. He had risked a lot in his search for the truth. The people he was investigating were not the sort to hesitate over the excising of someone getting too close to them.

Which was an odd thought, coming from the man who had shot him twice through the side of the head.

If Greeve had been given the contract before the book was published he might have wondered if there were a connection, if his masters were somehow implicated and wanted Castelle silenced, but it had been three months after publication when Heward called him in, and Castelle must have had the typescript in the hands of his publisher many months earlier, maybe as much as a year earlier, so the CIA or the DIA would have known what he had written and they might have told MI6. The secret intelligence agencies have a morbid fear of the public learning anything embarrassing about them and go to great lengths to keep tabs on what is due to be published and if necessary suppress it.

Greeve thought back to the two days he had spent with Heward in the hotel in Skegness. They had booked in separately, as always, and met as if by accident in the bar, as if they were strangers. Later, in Heward's room, Greeve had gone through the file on Hugo Castelle. Because of who he was there was no shortage of information.

'Why do you want him excised?' That was always the question Greeve wanted answered first.

'We found it difficult to believe, at first, but we've been watching him closely for a long time now and there's no doubt: Hugo Castelle is an Iraqi recruit. He spent two years in Iraq when he was younger.'

'Does that matter, these days? We beat them.'

'Yes, it matters. Iraq is a pot coming back to the boil. It matters especially when the recruit has Castelle's access to top people and high-grade information. He is also a respected writer – note the awards he's won – and a particularly influential propagandist. Have you read his books or his articles?'

'No. Never heard of him till today.' Greeve caught the tiny flicker of expression on Heward's face. To Heward he was still the surly army sergeant from a broken home, educationally limited and unimaginative. Greeve had never seen any reason to enlighten him. Heward was a snob and Greeve had never liked snobs.

'They're heavy going, but you could try reading his one about Irangate. He manages, very subtly, to make Reagan and North and Bush and the CIA and just about everyone else look like ruthless villains while Iraq comes out as a sleepy little country ruled by a benevolent father-figure. It's cleverly done.'

That wasn't the impression Greeve was getting from his belated reading of Castelle's book, but he supposed he had to make allowances for Heward's insider knowledge and his sense of what was right and wrong. Heward was a man with a very clear and straightforward ideology. In other days it might have been called Fascism.

Greeve walked as far as the end of the beach then turned and came back along the sheep-shorn grass above the concrete wall built to support and protect the roofless prehistoric houses of Skara Brae. He stopped and looked down into the circular stone-built dwellings. Everything was constructed from the local sandstone slabs: bed alcoves, dressers, shelves, hearths, pits for shellfish and grain.

He stood there for a long time, trying to imagine what

life must have been like four thousand years ago. The average age at death of the prehistoric inhabitants of Orkney was twenty-two.

He wondered why he was able to relate more deeply to these unknown people than to the men – and one woman – he had excised.

The weather on the Sunday was showery and windy and he passed the day reading and eating and drinking in a moderate way. In the afternoon he went out for a very fast walk over the fields and along the beach and up to the top of the cliffs and back to an hour of exercises before putting a steak pie in the oven and going for a shower. He prepared potatoes and peas and finished Lisa Castelle's book over the meal.

There was a lot of talent in the Castelle family. No doubt quite a lot of money as well.

He found it impossible to stop thinking about Lisa Castelle. Time and again he turned to the back of the dust jacket and studied her photograph intently, trying to imagine her face coming alive.

The daily papers don't reach Orkney till about 11 a.m. He drove into Kirkwall on the Monday morning and did his shopping at the supermarket and bought a *Glasgow Herald* and sat in a pub near the harbour and caught up on the news. Things like taxation and education and property prices don't mean much to a man who doesn't pay tax or have children or own a house, and his habit of moving around the world had given him a rather detached attitude towards the problems of any one country. He looked at the TV listings, hoping to find an old Randolph Scott movie showing during the afternoon, but there was nothing of interest. What he did find was that Lisa Castelle was to be interviewed on a book programme on Channel Four at 10.30 p.m.

The rain had cleared and he drove back by way of Rendall and Evie and Twatt. He loved that name. He wondered if there was still a post office in the wooden shed at Twatt; it would have been good to send someone a postcard saying, the message is on the postmark. But he didn't have any friends and he didn't know Heward's address, and he wouldn't have sent him a postcard anyway. They didn't have that kind of relationship.

He waited impatiently for 10.30 p.m. He wanted to see her and hear her voice.

The presenter was a rather too intense young man with designer stubble and a blue denim shirt with a sunburst tie.

'Good evening. My first guest tonight is Lisa Castelle, author of Casualties: The Vietnam Legacy. Miss Castelle, welcome.'

'Thank you.'

The picture changed from close-up to two-shot. Lisa Castelle was wearing a simple light-blue dress of some shiny material. Graceful bare arms, small waist, stunning legs. Greeve sat forward in his chair, staring.

'Reading your book, I got the impression that meeting the Vietnam veterans, gaining their confidence, getting their stories, must have been a harrowing experience.'

'It was. It was very difficult. I remember....'

The two-shot became a close-up and the face Greeve had studied so carefully in the photographs came alive. The tight curls had vanished and her hair lay soft and black on her shoulders, moving gently with her animation, the lights catching it. Her eyes were expressive and astonishingly beautiful, her lips full and made for smiling. Her voice was soft, clear, with only a slight West Coast accent. She spoke easily, coherently, confidently.

'Your father was, of course, Hugo Castelle. Was he a major influence in your life?'

'He made me want to be a writer. He taught me and

encouraged me and inspired me and read my first attempts and was very patient and somehow managed to show me how awful my writing was without actually destroying my confidence. When my first short story was published he read it and said it was quite good but that I'd telegraphed the ending and that I should have chosen a different point of view. I didn't discover till much later that afterwards he went out and boasted about me all over town.'

'He had a reputation for being a man with a … a permanent thirst, as it were.'

'He went into bars to talk to people. And to listen to people. Anyone. He loved people. The drinking just went with the talk.'

'He was murdered in a hotel in Marseille. No one was ever charged with the crime, and there is evidence of …'

'He was killed because he had uncovered facts he shouldn't have about illegal arms deals.'

'Irangate.'

'No, that was earlier. I think he was on to something else, something different.'

'Did he talk about his work?'

'Yes, sometimes. We sometimes didn't see each other for months at a time and I'm not completely sure what he was working on just before he was murdered, but he'd finished his book on Irangate and he was working on something new, something related, something he'd come across during his research. He told me that much.'

'There is evidence that he was involved in drugs….'

'My father was no angel, but he wasn't in the business of selling or importing drugs.'

'He'd used drugs….'

'He'd smoked pot. That was all. He was very anti-drugs. The fact that I've never so much as smoked a joint – and don't smoke at all – is entirely due to his influence.'

'So who killed him? And why?'

'I'm working on that.'

'*Do you mean ...?*'

'*I mean, my father was murdered to keep him quiet about something and I'm going to find out who did it and why.*'

'*Do you have any evidence?*'

'*I'd rather not say.*'

'*Your parents divorced when you were eighteen, I think.*'

'*Yes.*'

'*How did that affect you?*'

'*I could see it coming. Dad was one of those men who should never get married. He was a marvellous father but a lousy husband. The divorce didn't affect me much because I still saw them both. I still see my mother at least once a week when I'm in San Francisco. She's a marvellous woman. She's remarried and has gone back to writing.*'

'*You married at twenty-two and divorced at twenty-five. You're now twenty-seven....*'

'*I'll be twenty-eight in a couple of months.*'

'*You're beautiful and successful and a respected and award-winning writer, but I can't help wondering if what you have now is what you anticipated, say, ten years ago.*'

'*I didn't anticipate a bestselling book or the awards; I never expected my marriage to break up; I certainly never anticipated that my father would be murdered.*'

There was an uncomfortably long pause. It sounded as if the interviewer had realized Lisa Castelle was becoming increasingly impatient with the anodyne questions.

'*Do you still write fiction?*'

The interview continued for a few more minutes then the next guest was brought on to discuss his new biography. Lisa Castelle, and Greeve, had never heard of the subject, someone from the eighteenth century. He watched until the end of the programme but she appeared only for brief moments and said only a few more words.

He switched off and sat staring at her photograph.

There was something infinitely sad about the way she still believed her father was a hero, something childlike and fragile about her love for him. He hoped she would never learn the truth.

He phoned Heward from a call box beside the harbour in Stromness on the Wednesday afternoon.

'Mr Lomas, please. My name's Harry Hotspur.'

'I'm afraid you have a wrong number.'

'I'll wait till Shrove Tuesday.'

'You have a wrong number.'

'I'm calling in.'

Heward came on. 'Hello, Sergeant.'

'Any word from our customers in Switzerland?'

'There was activity. Everything's tidy.' That meant Playboy's own people had removed the bodies.

'There's a piece of equipment and some waste material in a hole in the ground which should be collected if possible.'

'Where?'

'Opposite the location, about a hundred yards up from the shore.'

'We'll take care of that.'

'Anything for me?'

'Possibly, Sergeant. We should meet. Where are you now?'

'Local, but there would be travel difficulties.' That meant in the UK but a long way from London.

'Call me again in an hour.'

'OK.'

Greeve went for a drink in the Ferry Inn then called Heward again an hour later and was given the name of a hotel in Lincoln and the name and address under which a room had been booked for him.

'It's for tomorrow night.'

'No problem. What's the deadline?'

'Uncertain. Whatever you're doing may have to be put on hold.'

'You're interrupting my holiday.'

'Charge it to expenses.'

'I will.'

Two contracts in one month. Killing seemed to be the country's only growth industry.

· Five ·

It was Greeve's first visit to Lincoln. He liked it. Maybe he'd come back some day and explore it properly. But in the winter, when it was quiet and cold.

He checked in at the hotel and rested for a while on the bed before going downstairs to the lounge bar. Heward was already there, behind his *Times*, aloof from the chatter of footsore tourists. Greeve bought a pint of cider and took the seat opposite him and noted the numbers 16 and 8 written lightly in pencil at the top right-hand corner of the front page. They didn't speak or even look at each other. Heward finished his whisky and left, taking the paper with him.

Greeve entered room 16 at precisely 8 p.m., locking the door behind him. Heward turned up the sound on the television and poured two glasses of whisky from a large hip flask. He pointed to a small spread of papers on the table by the curtained window and Greeve sat down and began to look through them.

'Bodo Roth,' Heward said, sitting close to him, his voice low. 'West German, age fifty-one. There's a lot about him we don't know, but what we do know is rather unpleasant.'

Greeve studied the two colour photographs. They were good quality enlargements, not too grainy. In one of them a fleshy man with carefully barbered grey hair and a lot of scalp showing was looking downwards, his soft mouth drooping in an expression of disapproval. In the other he wore a leather cap and was grinning at someone or something over his left shoulder. There was a square face under the jowls. His nose would be unmistakable, a real Karl Malden of a thing.

'Height a fraction under six feet, weight about sixteen stone. Badly out of condition. Smokes forty cigarettes a day plus a varying number of small cigars, drinks steadily but never seen drunk. Drives a red Passat. Lives with a coloured woman in a flat in Berlin: all the details are there.'

'Why do you want him excised?'

'He ostensibly earns his corn running a private detective agency, but that's just a cover. He makes his money as an intelligence broker; military, industrial and personal. He's been developing his contacts over the years and is now genuinely dangerous. He buys from anyone selling, sells to anyone buying. He is known, so people go to him, but he also chooses his targets. There's a distinct possibility he has started commissioning. A few weeks ago he was seen in the company of an Englishman who holds a senior position in a certain research establishment in Norfolk. Their meeting was not amicable. We got the impression the argument was about money. We know they are still in contact.'

'Interrogate your man from Norfolk.'

'That will happen when we're sure we have nothing more to gain from the situation.'

'So?'

'Roth plays very rough. We don't have proof we could present in court, but we're convinced – we know – he was responsible for the death of one of our people. A girl. Her talents lay rather more in being attractive than in being

clever. We had to get close to Roth and she was his type
so we risked it. We have no way of knowing quite what
went wrong, but she vanished. That was seven weeks
ago. There has been no sign of her since. We have to
assume the worst.'

'Revenge is hardly a good reason for a contract.'

'She was a family friend.'

'Still not a good reason.'

'Yes, it is.'

'No.'

'Dammit, Sergeant, I used my influence to get her the
job!'

'Your guilt isn't a good reason for a contract.'

Heward struggled to control his impatience. He had
always been resentful of the ex-sergeant's class-based lack
of proper respect for his superior officer, his unwarranted
questioning of orders, his mulish insistence on being
satisfied that the contracts were honourable.

'My masters would never countenance a revenge
killing. We want him dead because he's dangerous and
because we don't know just how far his grip extends. Kill
him and his whole network dies with him.'

Greeve shook his head. 'You don't inspire me.'

'It's just a bloody job, Sergeant! He's a nasty bit of work
and he killed one of our people and he's still operating.
We want him dead. If you don't do it I'll get someone
else.'

Greeve had often wondered if he were the only assassin
on the books. There had been a number of actions over
the years which bore all the marks of professional hits, but
it was hard to identify the people giving the orders.

He persisted, just to annoy Heward. 'Anger is the worst
possible motive.'

'I didn't come here to listen to a bloody lecture!'

'Keep your voice down.'

Heward emptied his glass and refilled it but without offering any to Greeve.

'Tell me more about him, Heward.'

The little man lay back on the bed and stared blindly into his glass, his polished brogues marking the patterned Downie.

'We didn't get on to Bodo Roth until about two years ago, but we estimate he's been operating for about twenty years. During that time he has probably cost this country several million pounds in lost intelligence and blown operations. Several million pounds and perhaps six lives. Counting Judy's. Indirectly, of course. He's stronger and more influential and more dangerous today than he ever was. Excising him would be effective and, I must admit, satisfying.'

Greeve decided it was time to stop playing Heward along. It was a minor indulgence and he knew he shouldn't do it.

'It's annual wage negotiation time.'

'Already?'

'It's been more than a year.'

Heward shrugged. 'Five percent?'

'Ten.'

'Seven and a half.'

'OK.' There was no fun in it when Heward gave in so easily. 'It's also brown envelope time.'

'On the chest of drawers there.'

Greeve took the big envelope and glanced inside. It was full of new £50 notes and represented his salary and premiums to date.

'By the way, why did you want me to read that article by Lisa Castelle?'

'It was relevant.'

'What does that mean?'

'She's looking for you.'

'But she's not going to find me.'

Heward hesitated. 'She may become a contract.'

'What?'

'We've been learning some surprising stuff about her. It's hard to be sure, and we're taking no action at this time, but.... Let's just say, it may turn out to be a case of like father, like daughter. Don't worry about it. The Cousins may take care of it.'

'Let me read this stuff.'

Heward sat and watched television for half an hour while Greeve read and memorized the data. When he eventually closed the file Heward looked at him and asked a question with his pale eyebrows. Over the years his fair hair had receded and he had finally given up growing one side long and combing it over to hide the male pattern baldness. Now he wore his hair quite short all over and looked much better. He had put on weight but he still wasn't fat.

Greeve nodded, meaning he accepted the contract.

'His address is here, but not the usual details about where to find him.'

'That's hard to answer. A very mobile target. We're running a watch on his flat and his office and another flat in Paris where he keeps a woman, and we're getting some information from the inside. We think the best thing would be for you to establish a base in Paris and we'll let you know when Roth is in the neighbourhood. The Berlin flat would be very difficult.'

Greeve had grown to like Paris. He had no objection to spending time there.

'Paris, then. Is he armed?'

'He's known to carry a small revolver of some kind; we don't know what.'

'Tell me about the flat in Paris.'

They talked for another hour and a half then Greeve left

and went out looking for a woman. He chose one but at the foot of the stairs he gave her £10 and apologized and said he wasn't feeling well. As he walked back to the hotel he managed to work it out.

The next time he made love to a woman it would be Lisa Castelle.

Greeve flew to Paris the following day and managed to find a room in a small commercial hotel near the Hospital des Peupliers. Bodo Roth's apartment was three streets away in a vaguely genteel terrace with little wrought-iron balconies overlooking the street. He contacted Heward and told him where he was and gave him his address and phone number. Then he set about getting to know the topography.

He had always liked this side of the job. He usually tried to come up with a minimum of five possible plans, which would then be narrowed down to two or three, which he then researched thoroughly and reduced to one, with one more as back-up. It meant having to move about as innocently as possible. On some jobs – Playboy, for instance – he tried to remain invisible, but this was one of the times when invisibility was not possible so he took the opposite tack and became someone people get used to very quickly, the enthusiastic Englishman in jeans and sandals and sunglasses, making a big thing of being an amateur artist in Paris for the first time, speaking schoolboy French and doing pathetic sketches and watercolours of the butcher's shop and the fountain and the trees in the Parc Montsouris. He stopped shaving and assumed an intent expression and pretended he thought the smiles were friendly rather than derisive.

He quickly identified Yvette Duvernet, Roth's mistress. He wondered if the German knew she was also spending a lot of time with the young man from the photocopying shop. He probably did. Bodo Roth was not naive. He probably didn't care.

Greeve decided on a plan of attack and called Heward.

'I'll need some gear.'

'Go on.'

'A small quiet one.' That meant a silenced automatic pistol. 'Doesn't matter much what: I expect to be working closely with the client. And a set of tweezers.' That meant picklocks.

Heward knew better than to suggest Greeve buy a gun locally. People talk. You can, with a little effort, buy just about any kind of weapon you want in any major city in the world, but it's not recommended if you're trying to keep a low profile. It was much easier to let Heward supply the necessary weapon from stock.

Greeve assumed he was like most professional assassins in having certain favourite weapons. But if you use the same kind of weapon too often you establish a pattern, an m.o., and the police computers start coughing out little reports and tiny scraps of information become associated with the hatchet man who always uses a Heckler and Koch P9S or whatever. A preference for certain types of location, certain types of cigarette, certain brands of soft drink, a certain standard of hotel, so on. Next thing you know there's a photofit picture on TV and after that your value to your masters takes a nosedive. So he rang the changes, never using the same weapon twice.

On the fifth day Heward called and reported that Roth had left Berlin by train and that he appeared to be on his way to Paris.

'Roth is a pro so we're not going to risk putting anyone on the train with him. If he arrives, good and well. If he doesn't, let me know. The samples you asked for should arrive any time now.'

Greeve had deliberately made himself a regular

customer at the café on the corner with a distant but clear view of the front door leading to Bodo Roth's apartment on the third floor of the block. He ordered coffee and made little sketches of the people in the street and waited; his sketching was actually becoming quite good by now. Roth arrived late in the afternoon, by taxi, looking hot and impatient.

When Greeve got back to the hotel there was a small parcel waiting for him. In it was a Walther PK5, a gun he'd never used before but which he knew to be thoroughly reliable. He stripped it and put it together again but someone had done that already, as always, and there were no problems. The silencer was small and neat and he hoped it would be efficient; he'd never liked suppressors. There were two full magazines. The small leather wallet with the zip contained a comprehensive selection of picklocks.

He shaved then bathed and dressed in a suit and blue shirt and tie and a corduroy cap and tinted glasses then went back out, the automatic loaded and tucked into the inside pocket of the jacket, the silencer in a trouser pocket. Bodo Roth's movements were not foreseeable: he might spend just an hour or two at his apartment then leave for some other destination or he could stay for a week. There was nothing Greeve could do but grab the chance as soon as it was presented.

Roth left the apartment just as the light was fading, accompanied by Yvette Duvernet. They walked two streets to a small restaurant and went inside. Greeve waited in a bar for a while then walked back to the apartment block, pulled on the thin leather gloves and went up the stairs and let himself in using the picklocks.

He toured the rooms then took up a position in a boxroom immediately inside the main door. He screwed the silencer on to the automatic and loaded it.

It was well after eleven before he heard the door being unlocked and the sudden murmur of voices. Lights came on. The sounds moved down the hall into the untidy sitting-room. The clink of glass on glass. Laughter.

He waited a few minutes then tied a large handkerchief across his face and replaced the tinted glasses. He slipped the safety catch on the automatic and walked silently out of the boxroom and approached the door of the sitting-room. It was slightly ajar. He could hear music, someone singing gently in French. He pushed the door slowly open with his foot and adopted the recommended police grip on the automatic and stepped halfway into the room.

Bodo Roth was sprawled on the couch, a glass in his hand, a small cigar in his mouth. Yvette Duvernet sat beside him, her head on his shoulder, a cigarette held like a pencil in one hand. As Roth turned his head to look at him Greeve double-tapped into his chest and again into the side of his head when he slumped.

The French girl drew breath to scream.

'Non! Silence!'

She froze. Greeve held the gun on her long enough for her to think about it and knew she would remain silent until he was well away. Then her eyes flicked to her right and he realized there was someone else in the room. He stepped to his right, ready to shoot, and saw Lisa Castelle rigid and terrified in an armchair.

Recognition was instant. Her head was turned towards him, the big dark eyes wide with horror, the beautiful mouth slightly open. The rich black hair was straight and gleamed in the light. Skinny-rib sweater, short skirt, dark stockings, black court shoes. The hand gripping the arm of the chair was slim and elegant, the nails not too long, varnished with a clear lacquer. Odd how you note all these things in a moment and are able to recall them later.

Greeve walked out of the apartment and raced down the stairs, unscrewing the silencer and tucking the automatic out of sight and ripping off the handkerchief before he walked casually out into the street and away, using the maze of openings and alleys and courtyards he had mapped out during the planning stage. He covered about half a mile then took a cab back to the hotel, to change quickly into the uniform of denims and sweat shirt then went back out and walked for six blocks before disposing of the automatic and the silencer in one dustbin off the Rue Bobillot, the suit and cap and gloves in another. Then he walked another mile and went into a bar and ordered cognac and lit a cigarette. He had a lot of thinking to do.

There wasn't much in the way of emotion in his life. Certainly not emotions like loving and caring and longing and missing. Coming right down to it, there really wasn't much in his life at all apart from occasional spells of fear and tension and then relief when a contract was completed. Being engrossed in the study of medieval armour or prehistoric Britain or the Impressionists hardly represented a full emotional life.

Perhaps that was why he had been hit so badly by finding Lisa Castelle with Bodo Roth. He guessed he felt the way a husband does when he finds his wife in bed with another man.

Which was ridiculous, of course. He'd never met the woman. He'd seen her picture, watched her on television, thought about her far too much. He had even, embarrassingly, decided she would be the next woman he made love to.

After the fourth cognac he reached the stage of making excuses for myself. Emotional immaturity, he decided, was to blame for this juvenile behaviour.

After the fifth cognac he'd decided it was all her fault.

After the sixth he knew he was infatuated by her.

· Six ·

Greeve got back to the hotel about one in the morning, keeping clear of the police activity. He wasn't stopped or questioned. He stayed at the hotel until the end of the week – because the one way he might have drawn attention to himself was by vanishing suddenly – then left and flew back to London. He waited until the Monday then called Heward at the usual time.

'Yes, Sergeant.'

'I've tied up that contract.'

'I know. Well done. Any problems?'

'Our friend wasn't alone.'

'I know. His social secretary was with him. It was in the Paris papers.' Heward never missed an opportunity to let Greeve know he was way ahead of the hired help. Which was why Greeve always enjoyed proving him wrong.

'There was someone else. You may know her: her father was one of our customers some time back. Writes a bit.'

A pause while Heward thought about that.

'You're certain of this?'

'Yes.'

'There was no mention of her in the papers.'

'She was there.'

Greeve waited. Heward was one of those people who

make you wait.

'Do you think she'll remember you?' Meaning, could Lisa Castelle identify him?

'No.'

'You're sure?'

'I'm sure.'

'Any idea why she was there?'

'No.'

Another pause. 'Oddly enough, Sergeant, this may be confirmation of what we've suspected for some time now. It may be that the young lady is carrying on her father's business.'

It was hard to accept but you can't argue with the facts. Lisa Castelle, like her father, was taking money from the Iraqis for services rendered. The best spies are the ones everyone *wants* to believe are innocent.

'I'll look into this, Sergeant. Call me.'

Greeve took a bedsitter in Chiswick and tried to cheer himself up by calling at the London branch of the Swiss bank and getting a copy of his statement. He knew he was no financial genius, but over the years the expenses had been generous and the savings had built up and he'd taken advice and invested carefully and by now there was a healthy sum of money tucked away where no one could find it. Some day soon he would retire and reappear under yet another name and settle down and stop killing people.

Maybe. He'd been thinking about it for years, usually immediately after a contract.

But he felt like it now. Finding Lisa Castelle in that room with Bodo Roth had hit him hard. Heward's information had been correct. No matter how much he wanted to deny the fact, Lisa Castelle was one of the nasties.

Even so, he hoped desperately that she would not

become a contract.

He knew he was reacting wildly; he knew he would calm down after a while and start thinking logically.

He went out for a woman, remembering his idiotically quixotic decision that the next woman he made love to would be Lisa Castelle. Afterwards, while he dressed, the woman lit a cigarette and scowled at him.

'You'd enjoy it more if you weren't in such a bad mood, luv.'

'I'll bear that in mind.'

Lacey arrived at the hotel and went upstairs and Rossi let him in. Carver was sprawled in an armchair in a bathrobe, a half-pint silver mug of champagne in his hairy fist, watching television. Even now he wore one of his wigs, the grey one parted on the left.

'Hey, my man!'

'I've been trying to get you all day.'

'I've been in New York. Just got in.'

'We should have a talk about things.'

'No sweat. I'll order dinner.'

'Not steak. I've had enough steak to last me the rest of my life.'

'What, then?'

'Fish. Seafood or trout or salmon.'

'You're on.' Carver nodded to the bodyguard; Rossi picked up the phone.

'So what's new, my friend?'

'My man has excised Bodo Roth. Lisa Castelle was there. I've sown the seeds of suspicion.'

'Sown the seeds of suspicion. Jeez, I like that! Sown the seeds of suspicion. I love the way you talk, my friend.'

Lacey had never been quite sure of Carver's feeling towards him. He liked to think the continual joking and the sly digs were a sign of affection, perhaps even an indication of Carver's respect for his breeding and education. Carver had come up the hard way, from a poor Texas farm through a job with a wholesale arms dealership in Dallas to his present position. There was no doubt the American was intelligent and shrewd; perhaps intelligent enough and shrewd enough to recognize that his abilities as a wheeler-dealer still left him a long way short of a man with public school and Cambridge behind him.

'I see it as a game of chess,' Lacey said. He remembered Carver confessing to not understanding chess. 'The question is, do we want Lisa Castelle excised? It will raise a stink. The fact that her father was excised will be remembered and comparisons will be drawn. Conspiracy theories will be aired. People will ask what she and her father had in common and someone may come up with the correct answer: they were both investigating illegal arms dealing. Do you want that?'

Carver emptied the mug and refilled it. 'We don't know how much she's learned. Her father managed to track down four or five people on the fringe of the operation and I must assume she knows what her father knew. She has spoken to another two or three. They are people who know only their own tiny part in the scheme of things.'

'So?'

'So it's a case of which is worse for us – the reaction to Lisa Castelle being killed, or the consequences if she's not killed.' Carver shrugged his massive shoulders. 'This is your area of expertise, my friend. This is why I pay you.'

'Is that a go-ahead?'

'Let me think about it. I fancy some tail. Want some?'

Carver's abrupt changes of subject could still catch Lacey flat-footed.

'Well....'

'Rossi, call Mrs Norman. Tell her we'll be round later

and that one of the gentlemen will require a coloured lady. Right, my friend?'

Lacey nodded, embarrassed but excited.

On the Monday Greeve set to work on the task of locating Lisa Castelle.

He bought yet another copy of her book and checked through it and chose the name Colin Sinclair because he had a passport in the name of Alan Sinclair. Then he moved to a different bedsitter, calling himself Alan Sinclair, and phoned her London publishers and said he wanted to get in touch with her. They provided the name of the firm of literary agents in New York who acted for her, and the affiliates in London. He called the London number and was put on to a rather brisk woman.

'My name's Alan Sinclair. I'd like to get in touch with Lisa Castelle.'

'Why, Mr Sinclair?'

'I've just read her book about the Vietnam veterans and there's a possibility one of the men she met, Colin Sinclair, may be my cousin. We lost touch many years ago.'

'I see. And what do you want from Miss Castelle?'

'She honoured her commitment to those men: she didn't reveal where they are. I was hoping she might give me Colin's address, or if that's not possible, write to him enclosing a letter from me. I'd like to offer him a holiday with me, maybe even a home.'

'I see. She lives in San Francisco, of course, but she's in Europe just now, doing research. I don't know exactly where she is at the moment.'

'Does she keep in touch with you?'

'She calls occasionally, yes.'

'I'd give you my number, but I travel a lot. May I leave my address and you could pass it on to her and explain the reason for my interest?'

'Yes, of course.'

It meant staying on in Chiswick for a while, but it was worth it. He passed the time broadening his education; this time he went back to a favourite subject, the Impressionists. On the following Monday the landlady brought in a letter with his eggs and bacon. It had been written on a word processor with a dot matrix printer. Only the signature was handwritten, in a strong upright script.

Dear Mr Sinclair

My agents in London have advised me of your call. If you write to Colin care of them I'll collect your letter next time I'm in London and will forward it to him as soon as possible. As I said in my book, he is a fine man but shattered by his experiences in Vietnam and now lives as a recluse in a remote part of Oregon. I doubt very much if he would be interested in a vacation in England, and I have to say it would almost certainly be a mistake, perhaps a dangerous mistake, to take him into your home. But that's your decision, and his. Just don't get too optimistic.

Best wishes

Lisa Castelle

The content of the letter didn't matter much, nor did the fact that she hadn't dated it or shown an address at the top. What mattered was that, although she had used plain A4 typing paper, she had enclosed the letter in an envelope bearing the name and address of a hotel in Aix-en-Provence.

Greeve visited the bank in the City and was taken downstairs to the safe deposit vault, left the passports he'd used in Paris and took out the one in the name of Alan Sinclair and a couple of spares from his extensive collection, along with the matching papers to back up the legends. He caught a plane that afternoon, reflecting that Aix-en-Provence was only a short drive from Marseille, where he had excised Lisa Castelle's father.

As he watched the Channel pass under the wind he was suddenly very aware that he was breaking all his own rules in seeking her out. There was a distinct possibility that any time now he might be called to meet Heward in a hotel somewhere, to be shown a file with Lisa Castelle's picture in it and then Heward would motivate him and he would track her down and excise her. The sense of urgency he felt, the way he kept refusing to think of her as a nasty, the way he was forever looking at her photograph on the back of the dust jacket of her book, the way he could recall her soft Californian voice, the way he could remember her smooth skin and terrified eyes and long fingers, all this suggested he was the victim of a puerile crush, an immature infatuation, a ridiculous compulsion.

All he knew was that he had to meet Lisa Castelle. He had to see her and talk to her and be close to her. He had to see her eyes looking directly at his and hear her voice and watch her lips and admire the way her hair lay on her shoulders.

As for the rest of her....

He could still close his eyes and picture her sitting in the armchair in Bodo Roth's apartment in Paris, half-turned towards him, slim legs shapely in dark stockings, breasts rounded under the tight jersey, not too big, not too small. He could still feel, intensely, his own reaction: she wasn't fragile, but she needed his protection. She was not overtly glamorous but she was beautiful and electrifying and fascinating.

She was divorced, but that didn't mean she was alone.

No one that beautiful is ever alone. Maybe she had someone with her now, an American or a Frenchman or just a man. Maybe she screwed around.

Jesus H. Christ! He was jealous of men who might not exist because maybe they were sleeping with a woman he'd never met!

He shook his head in futile despair at his own pathetic emotional foolishness but at the same time he knew he was going to take this thing all the way.

It was some kind of compulsion. He knew it but assumed he would be able to control it.

Lisa Castelle probably didn't have to count the pennies, but at the same time she didn't throw the stuff around. The hotel in Aix-en-Provence was a three-star affair, a straggling old building on the edge of the town with a rather cramped car-park at the back. Greeve had phoned ahead from the airport and they had been able to find him a single room, no shower, at the rear. He parked the rented Peugeot and took the case and the flight bag inside and checked in.

'I'm hoping to meet a Miss Castelle. Is she still staying here?'

The pretty receptionist smiled knowingly.

'Yes, m'sieu. I think she's out at the moment.'

'Thank you.'

He went up to his room and showered in the bathroom at the end of the corridor, changed and went downstairs to explore. It was now the end of the first week in September and the day had been bright but windy and the temperature was bearable. He wandered through the lounge and the hall and the television room and the bars but there was no sign of her. He settled himself in a corner of a bar and ordered a beer but he had to wait until halfway through dinner before she appeared.

She was alone. She looked cool and fresh and stunning in a simple but probably expensive off-white cotton dress with a matching jacket and a wide blue belt which emphasized her small waist. He was surprised at how tiny she was; she couldn't have been more than 5'2'' in her flat-soled blue shoes.

Heads turned and she was aware of the effect she was creating but she ignored it. She sat with her back to the room and ordered and read from a large notebook while she ate. Greeve left the dining-room before her and waited over coffee in the lounge, watching the door. When she came in and sat down he rose and walked over.

'Miss Castelle? I'm Alan Sinclair. You very kindly wrote to me a few days ago.'

He watched the big dark eyes for any hint of recognition, but all he saw was momentary annoyance then surprise.

'I remember. But ...'

'What am I doing here?'

'Yes.'

'It's no mystery. May I sit down for a moment? I promise I won't take up too much of your time.'

He sat opposite and leaned back, not crowding her, and persisted with the polite, slightly diffident approach.

'The envelope you used had the name of this hotel on it. I had planned a visit to Nice later in the week; I just flew down a couple of days early and took a chance on meeting you.'

'You're lucky: I'm probably moving on tomorrow.' A slight warning in the words: don't get too friendly, I'm just leaving.

'All I need is a few minutes of your time. To ask you about Colin. When I got your letter I suddenly realized my idea of wanting to look after him might be a mistake.'

'Yes, I think it would be.' She clasped her hands

between her knees and hunched her shoulders and inclined slightly towards him. The body language was looking good. She was ready to confide in him; she had accepted him.

'It took me three weeks to get Colin to trust me enough to say a few words. It took me another two weeks to get to the stage of being able to ask him about Vietnam. It took me six more weeks to drag the story out of him.'

Greeve watched intently, only half-listening to the words. Her photograph and her image on the television screen hadn't done her justice. Her skin was very fine-textured, very slightly olive, unblemished. He wondered for a moment if the long dark eyelashes were artificial, but they weren't; when the soft lips parted she revealed strong white teeth. She was wearing no cosmetics, because she didn't need them: she had nothing to hide and nothing needed to be exaggerated or enhanced. The dark eyes were lively and fascinating, the whites very white. He found himself wanting to change the subject to something lighter so he could see her smile.

'In all that time I never saw him without a hunting rifle in his hand and an automatic pistol in a holster and a huge knife in a sheath. He is one very dangerous and spaced-out guy. He lives in the backwoods because he knows that if he lived among people he would flip and kill someone. He spent two years in a veterans' hospital, you know.'

'I know. I've read the chapter about him many times.'

'You said he's your cousin?'

'I'm fairly sure he might be.' Greeve had worked it all out on the plane. 'My father's half-brother emigrated to the States just after the war. World War Two, I mean. There wasn't a lot of family feeling between my father and Colin's father, but they did write occasionally. Several of the facts you mentioned – a Scots father, Delaware, a small business – all these point to Colin being my cousin. And his appearance – tall, sandy hair, freckles – my father's brother looked like that.'

'I talked to Colin's father. He looks nothing like that. He's actually dark-haired and not too tall.'

'Oh.' Greeve acted out a man experiencing dashed hopes. It didn't really matter much if the long-lost cousin story collapsed now. It had been nothing more than a way of gaining an introduction and a measure of trust.

'I'm sorry, Alan. I can see you're disappointed.'

'It was a long shot, I suppose. It's just....'

'What?'

'My mother died years ago; my father died eight months ago; I've no other family. I suppose I just felt lonely.'

'I know how you feel.'

She was supposed to know how he was pretending to feel. He was still working on building common ground between them. He gave her a sympathetic look.

'I remember. You lost your father, didn't you? He was....'

'Murdered. In Marseille. Just a few miles from here.' She stared at him, her beautiful eyes narrowed with hate. 'Some day I'll find the bastard who did it. And then I'll make him suffer.'

· **Seven** ·

Greeve was fascinated by the hands holding the coffee cup. A pianist's hands, or at least the idealized concept of a pianist's hands, slender and graceful and sensitive. He wondered how it would feel to have Lisa Castelle's hands caressing his body and felt a tingle of reaction at the thought.

He smiled ruefully. 'I've a friend who has three brothers and a sister, all married with children. When I visit him he apologizes for all the noise and the arguments and kids running around and chaotic meals and so on. He doesn't believe me when I say that's what I love about being in his house.'

Lisa smiled and instinctively Greeve smiled back. He wasn't acting now. Her smile was the kind you'd like to see every day of your life. He wanted to make her so happy she would smile all the time.

'Are you married, Alan?'

'No. Almost was, once, but I took cold feet. She was the sort of girl who would make an excellent manager. I'm old-fashioned enough to want the responsibility of looking after a wife and children and a home rather than being a member of the staff.'

He wasn't quite sure why he'd said that. He should have been less definite about his attitudes until he'd learned what she preferred in a man, but something about her prompted him to blurt out the truth. Linda was a long time ago, while he was still in the Army, but he hadn't forgotten her.

'I get the impression you're a rather lonely man, Alan.'

It was an opportunity to gain a little sympathy. Greeve shrugged and made a dismissive face, to indicate he wasn't looking for sympathy.

'I'm in control of my life. Whatever I am is my own choice. Maybe I prefer relationships rather than marriage and a long-term commitment. Maybe my own parents' circumstances influenced me. I don't know. They divorced eventually, but they should have done it years earlier. They stayed together for my sake, but all that did for me was to make me aware of the screaming tension that can exist between a man and a woman.'

Lisa Castelle nodded her head slowly. 'My folks divorced too, but I come from a society where divorce is so common you half expect it to happen. It was still a bit of a jolt for all that. At least I still see my mother regularly. What line are you in?'

'What?' Greeve had been momentarily distracted by the discovery that she wasn't wearing stockings; she seemed to be the same delicious colour all over. 'Line?'

'Work. Profession.'

'I see.' He dropped automatically into the story he had prepared years before, the one which couldn't be checked, the one he could back up from his continuing fascination with French nineteenth century painting and his very good visual memory.

'I suppose you could say I'm a private collector who sells his collection. Dad was a natural money-maker – he was in the City – but I rather loused up my education and abused his generosity and never settled to any particular trade. I suppose I was something of a parasite, really – I drank too much and smoked the wrong things and screwed around. But I knew I was going bad and sorted that out before I did too much damage and started relying on my ability to spot a decent work of art before anyone else did. It all began quite accidentally when I saw a small painting in a junk shop. It was filthy and someone had put a cheap modern frame on it but something told me it was special and I bought it for two pounds. It was a Cézanne, one of his Mont Sainte-Victoire pictures. I sold it for nine thousand. I've been buying and selling ever since. I make a good living and enjoy the travel.'

'You have a gallery?'

Greeve shook his head. 'I don't even have a home, really. Used to have, but it was empty half the year, so now I just rent rooms wherever I happen to be.'

'Sounds fascinating. Are you on the trail of something now?'

'Is this the journalist at work?' He smiled to let her know he wasn't really objecting to her questions and she grinned, making tiny lines beside her mouth.

'Sorry. I didn't realize that's how it sounded. I'm honestly not trying to get your secrets out of you.'

'There are no secrets. It's not as if I'm tracking down a missing Van Gogh or whatever. I'm on holiday, going to visit old friends. But I keep my eyes open wherever I go. How about you? Your agent in London said you were doing research.'

The animation vanished from her face and Greeve regretted spoiling the moment. He wanted her relaxed and in a good mood.

'My father was murdered in Marseille. The police said it was a drug-related killing, which is nonsense. He's now labelled as a someone who used his influence and status as a famous journalist and author to carry heroin and that's a foul lie and I'm going to prove it.'

She looked steadily into the eyes of her father's killer.

'I'm going to nail the shit who murdered Dad if it's the last thing I do.'

There was an awkward pause in the conversation. Greeve wondered if she felt embarrassed by her own display of ferocity, and was himself rather at a lost for words. You get that way, he decided, chatting to the daughter of someone you've murdered.

'Is that why you're here, Lisa? So close to Marseille, I mean?'

'I've been talking to people, trying to get the facts. I'm hoping there may be a book in it, or at least a series of articles, but finding the killer takes precedence over everything else.'

Greeve raised his hands apologetically. 'It must sound as if I'm doing the prying now. I'm not. Would you like a cognac?'

'I'd rather have a liqueur. Drambuie, if they have it.'

He took care of that and more coffee. 'I saw you reading your notebook over dinner. Research?'

'Yes. Lots of notebooks; page after page of scraps of information. Tell me about some of your successes. Your paintings, I mean.'

Greeve made up a story about finding a Monet in a cardboard box of trashy paintings and photographs at a house sale in Wales and having to bid against a lady who wanted the frames for her own appalling watercolours.

'The Monet was one he must have done at the same time as he did the San Giorgio Maggiore in Venice. In fact, it's almost exactly the same view, but at a different time of day. I got the whole box for ten quid and sold them to the lady for a fiver after extracting the Monet, so she was quite happy. Took me home with her for tea and the grand tour of her collection of watercolours. Her measure of artistic success was the number of paintings she could do at one sitting. Her tea was strong enough to stain your teeth and her scones were like lead sinkers. It was a rough day.'

'But profitable, presumably.'

'Certainly. Enough to pay my wages for the year.'

'I'd love to own a great painting. Just one. Something by Van Gogh, maybe.'

'Say it *Goch*, as in *loch*.'

'Not *Goff*?'

'No.'

'I'll remember, although I may not manage it. Thank you.'

'I like your reaction. A lot of people object to having their pronunciation corrected.'

'I don't. Dad taught me to be grateful to anyone who teaches me something I don't know.'

'He sounds like a nice guy to have as a father.'

'He was. The best. I miss him.'

'If he wasn't involved in drugs, why was he murdered?'

Her eyes flickered to his and away again. 'I don't know.'

'You're lying, Lisa.'

Her face tightened and he made his point before she could speak.

'It doesn't matter. I had no right to ask and I've a feeling you're being careful. Whoever killed him may be afraid you'll get too close to the truth. You could be in danger.'

She exhaled slowly and her body relaxed. She would probably be a tiger when she was angry.

'Yes, I was lying. And you seem to understand why.' She paused for a moment, sipping the Drambuie, coming to a decision about how far she could trust him. 'I was talking to a man in Paris a few days ago; Bodo Roth; he was a man my father had talked to while he was researching his book on Irangate. Have you read it?'

'Yes.'

'He's mentioned in chapters six and seven; Dad called him The Detective. While I was with this man, actually sitting in the same room as him, he was murdered.'

'What?'

'Murdered. It was horrifying. We'd met by arrangement in a restaurant, Roth and his mistress and I, then we'd walked back to his apartment; he was sitting on a couch with Yvette beside him and I was in an armchair. We were drinking Calvados and there was music and he was being amusing about an argument he'd had with a cab driver. Then I saw his face change and looked up and there was a man standing there with a gun in his hand and a mask over his face and dark glasses and thin leather gloves. He didn't say anything. He just coldly and efficiently and mercilessly shot Bodo Roth twice in the chest and twice more in the head.'

Greeve shook his head to indicate his inability to comprehend how anything like this could happen.

'Did he threaten you?'

'No. He shouted at Yvette to keep quiet, pointed the gun at her and then at me, paused for a moment then walked out. I suppose he'd had his orders to kill Bodo Roth and we weren't in the contract. But I must admit I thought my time had come.'

'What did the police say to all this?'

'I don't know. I didn't want my name associated with what had happened, in case it stopped people talking to me. I managed to convince Yvette – we were both rather hysterical – that there was no sense complicating the story with my being there, then I slipped away before she called the police and before she could get her brain in gear.'

'Could you recognize this man again?'

'There was nothing to recognize except his clothes. He was a male Caucasian, that's all. A bit taller than you, perhaps. A professional.'

'But he didn't kill you.'

'Not that time. But suppose he reports back to someone that I was there with Bodo Roth? Suddenly I'm a potential danger to them, whoever they are. So you can see why I'm less than honest with you. Or anyone.'

'Maybe you should just give up, go home, write something else. I'd hate to open my paper some morning and read that you'd been found murdered. That would be a terrible waste of someone so ... well, someone so lovely and vital and intelligent. Sorry.'

She laughed. 'You're very English. You pay a lady a compliment then apologize and look embarrassed.'

'It's something to do with our upbringing. It also has something to do with the fact that in England ladies don't know how to accept compliments.'

'I know. It's worse in the States. A compliment is assumed to be a lead-in to a proposition.'

She was anxious to get away from the subject of her father and why he had been murdered, and if Greeve had persisted in trying to get her to talk it would have looked suspicious. He went with the flow. They talked for the best part of an hour about writing and life in California and the art market and so on then she picked up her notebook and gave him a smile.

'It's been fun talking to you, Alan, but I must go. I have a couple of phone calls to make and then I'll have to work out what to do next.'

'Are you moving on tomorrow?'

'I won't know till I make the calls. There's someone I've been trying to get hold of for a week, but he's been away.'

'Perhaps I'll see you at breakfast.'

'Perhaps.'

He rose with her. 'I really would like to see you again, Lisa. If you want to.'

'We'll see. Good night.'

'Good night.'

He moved to the bar and sat for a time over a cognac, thinking about Lisa Castelle, wondering what to do next. All the thinking about her he'd done, all the staring at photographs and watching her on television and fantasizing about her, all that hadn't prepared him for the effect she would have on him. She was stunning. He was stunned. All the women he'd met over the years had suddenly become nonentities. He knew that for the rest of his life any woman but her would be second-best. Tenth-best.

It couldn't end here and now, after just a short time spent with her in a French hotel lounge. Whatever happened, whatever the problems, it had to continue. He had to spend more time with her, get her to feel something for him, get her into bed, make himself the man she would spend the rest of her life loving.

How had she reacted to him? He had performed his act reasonably well. He had created a persona she could respond to; he had managed to prevent himself coming on too strongly; he had displayed good manners and intelligence and a sense of humour and some strength of character. He had deliberately accused her of lying, hoping this would have the correct effect, hoping it would show her he was direct and honest. And at the end he had indicated his interest in her but without being too aggressive or blatant.

All he could do now was wait and see what happened. He wanted her to make the next move.

Everything would depend on whether or not she did what he hoped she would do – distrust him.

She joined him at the breakfast-table. She wore faded blue denims and a blue chambray shirt and white canvas shoes and looked good enough to eat. Greeve rose politely as she approached and gave her the diffident smile.

'You look very cheerful this morning.'

'Yes. Success at last. I managed to get hold of that guy I mentioned and I'm going to see him this morning. And I made another call and you'll be glad to know you're off the hook.'

'Sorry?'

'Your address was still in my word processor. I called your landlady, Mrs Beattie.'

Greeve looked momentarily puzzled. 'To check up on me?'

'Of course.'

He made a show of thinking about that then smiled and nodded in approval. 'You had to be sure I wasn't a plant, someone connected with the people who killed your father.'

'Exactly. Offended?'

'I could be. I prefer to be flattered by your interest. She couldn't have had much to say: I had the room for only a week.'

'You made an impression. *"That nice Mr Sinclair? Him with his painting books and his questions"?'* Her attempt at a Cockney accent was way off. ' *"Any good junk shops in the neighbourhood? Did I know anyone who had lots of paintings? But a lovely man, dearie; bought me a nice bunch of flowers when he left".'*

His groundwork was paying dividends.

'I'll stay with her again some time. She does a glorious steak and kidney pie. So you'll be staying on here for a while?'

Lisa nodded. 'Another day, anyway.'

'Fine. Could we meet this evening? I'll find a good restaurant.'

'That's a definite maybe. I should be back by then. If I'm going to be late I'll call you.'

Greeve watched from the dining-room window as she drove away. Another rented Peugeot, red, small dent over the rear offside wheel arch. He automatically memorized the registration number.

There was nothing to indicate she was under surveillance. He had been alert to that possibility ever since deciding to go looking for her in France. If Heward considered her a possible nasty then it followed that he would order an investigation, but it would take time to set that up. He had often complained about the problems of a tight budget. If he put a tail on her he would learn within a matter of hours that Greeve was with her and it wasn't difficult to guess his reaction.

Greeve spent the morning wandering around Aix-en-Provence, visiting the galleries and museums, looking at paintings, then after lunch worked on his legend by seeking out as many junk shops and stalls as he could find. It would have been perfect if he could have spotted an unrecognized work by one of the great artists, but of course that didn't happen. What he did find was a pastel drawing of a nude, her back to the artist. It was unsigned and in poor condition, one corner missing, but the dealer claimed it was a Degas. Greeve thought he might be correct but insisted he was wrong. They both lied effortlessly for a while and eventually agreed a figure of just over £50.

Then he chose a restaurant, booked a table and bought a pack of condoms.

They met in the bar at the hotel. Tonight she was wearing a tight dress in dark-red silk, knee-length, the skirt flared from the hips, with matching high-heeled shoes and a silk stole over her shoulders. She had used lipstick and eye shadow and put her hair up in a loose arrangement which made her look completely different.

The bar went silent when she came in and he couldn't help feeling the thrill of possession when she joined him and sat down. A waiter appeared like magic and they ordered.

'You look magnificent.'

'Thank you. I felt like putting on the dog a bit, to cheer myself up.'

'Why do you need cheering up?'

'My own fault. I expected more from my contact than actually happened. How about you? Find any long-lost masterpieces?'

'I found a tatty little pastel which I think may be a Degas. It's a present for you. I'll give it to you later.'

'You're going to give me an original Degas? Oh, come on, Alan, this is too much.'

'It *may* be a Degas, and if it is he probably used it as a coaster after tearing off one corner to make a toothpick. It's just a sketch, unsigned. A curio of no great intrinsic value. More the sort of thing a gentleman gives to a lady in the hope that she will form a good opinion of him.'

'I've already formed a good opinion of you.'

'Oh. Does that mean I've wasted a dollar fifty?'

There was more in her laughter than amusement. He knew then he'd be using the condoms.

· Eight ·

They took a taxi to the restaurant. It was a noisy and cheerful place, the food first-class, the service friendly. Lisa ate and drank with appreciation and appetite. They stayed clear of the subject of her father and her investigation, preferring to keep the mood light. They found a variety of common interests, including the films of Woody Allen, and her impression of Diane Keaton as Annie Hall was a lot more accurate than her attempt at Mrs Beattie of Chiswick. The people at the next table actually applauded.

The mood when they returned to the hotel was quieter but still relaxed and intimate. Greeve was sure she had already made up her mind about what was to happen next.

'I'll go up and get your Degas.'

'I'm in room 21. I'll leave the door open.'

He freshened up and went back downstairs and let himself in. The red silk dress was lying over a chair and she was in the bathroom. He locked the door behind him. When she came out she was wearing a white towelling robe and had loosened her hair and removed the make-up.

He handed her the pastel in its polythene envelope.

'I did say it was in poor condition.'

'You really think it's a Degas?'

'Yes, I do.'

'It's beautiful. Thank you, Alan. I'll treasure it.'

She put one hand round his neck and pulled his head down and kissed him. In her bare feet the top of her head was level with his chin. Her lips were soft and warm and she smelled of soap and talc and woman. He took her head in his hands, gently, and made her thank-you kiss into a lover's kiss and she did not resist.

He took the pastel from her hand and placed it on the bedside cabinet. She waited calmly. He pushed the hair back from her face and kissed her again and put his arms round her and brought her in close. Her body was so slim and yet so strong. She held on to his shoulders and gave herself up to the moment, her breath fanning his cheek, her mouth as eager as his. He heard her tiny grunt of pleasure.

What should be a magic moment is always spoiled by the problem of undressing. You can't do it gracefully. All you can do is do it. They parted and he unbuttoned his shirt and pulled it off.

'I knew you'd be like this.' She ran her fingertips down his chest. It was like being touched by fire. 'I knew you'd be lean and hard.'

She watched while he got rid of the rest of his clothes. There seemed no point in modestly retaining his briefs. He was already semi-erect. The sound of her breathing quickened. He loosened the belt of her robe and opened it and slipped it off her shoulders and let it drop. She was wearing a small cream-coloured bra, a simple affair, unwired, almost transparent, and he could see the brown circles of her nipples. Her skin was smooth and olive, unmarked except for one tiny brown mark close to her navel. Her stomach was beautifully rounded, her waist narrow, the curve to the hips a delight. Her panties were tiny, little more than a gesture towards propriety. A fine shadow of dark hair showed between them and the base of her belly. From where he was looking her pubic bulge was full and exciting.

She reached behind her back and the bra fell away. Perfect breasts, round and firm. He caressed the tips of the stiffening nipples with the palms of his hands and she closed her eyes and shivered and moaned gently. He did that for a time, mesmerized by the sensation, then dropped to his knees and cupped her taut buttocks with his hands and pulled her against his face, kissing the silk of her panties, moving his cheek against the smooth skin of her thighs, catching her scent, feeling her thrust against him, feeling her hands gripping his hair.

He hooked his fingers in the waistband of her panties and pulled them down to her ankles. Soft, dark pubic hair, not curly, not much of it. She moved her legs apart and her hands went to the back of his head, pulling him in, her hips pushing against his face. He used his tongue on her tiny erection and heard her gasping for breath and took her all the way. She climaxed quickly, her body arching, her grip in his hair marvellously painful, then sank slowly until she was crouched before him on her knees, her hair in a tangle across her face.

She took his erection in her hands and dropped her head. He let her do it for a minute or two then stopped her, with difficulty.

'Not that way, Lisa.'

'Yes.'

'No.'

He rose and lifted her and laid her on the bed. She was light and at that moment he felt very strong; she seemed to weigh nothing at all. He parted her legs and knelt between them and rolled the condom into position. She watched, her hands stroking her breasts and stomach, her eyes hooded, smiling the way women do when they've had it once and know they're going to get it a second time.

He went into her slowly, an inch and out again, two inches and out again, lubricating himself, not hurrying the moment. She was tight and muscular and eager for it and she wanted him to remember the occasion. She stroked his back and dragged her nails up and down the base of his spine and gripped with her thighs and the excitement of his orgasm made her climax again.

When he got his breath back he rolled off her and she turned and lay against him and they caressed each other, prolonging the pleasure. He couldn't get enough of the feel of her breasts. She sucked and bit his nipples and stroked his belly and fondled his balls and the base of his cock. He got rid of the condom and they kissed and lay there, cooling off.

She giggled. 'That was my first vertical orgasm. I thought Englishmen were supposed to be so conventional.'

'You must have screwed around with the wrong Englishmen.'

'I haven't screwed around with any Englishmen. In fact, it's a long time since I screwed around with any kind of man.'

'What's your idea of a long-time? Twenty-five minutes?'

'I could take offence at that. More than a year.'

'I don't believe you. No one as beautiful and exciting and randy as you could possibly go that long without attracting a lot of attention.'

'Some attention. No screwing.'

'Why not?'

'After Dad was murdered it just didn't seem right for a while and then I kind of got out of the habit. I've been a bit obsessive and there haven't been as many approaches as there used to be.'

'Sorry. I shouldn't have brought back bad memories.'

'It's all right.'

'But what about before that?'

'You know I'm divorced?'

Greeve couldn't remember if he was supposed to know about her divorce. 'So?'

'I married at twenty-two, divorced at twenty-five. It was a mistake from the start. We'd been lovers for a whole month and I thought it would always be like that. It wasn't.'

'Who was he?'

'A college professor. Brilliant, intense, very flip. A bore. His world was about eight feet wide. He'd been in school since he was four years old and he's still there. There's no one quite as shallow as an American academic. Every word he said had been written by someone else. Every word he wrote was a quote from some approved text. It was like living with a footnote in gold-rimmed glasses.'

'You sound bitter.'

'It was wasted time. I hate wasting time. I wanted to write something serious but he talked me out of it. Said my degree wasn't good enough for anything serious. Said I should stick to writing short stories and magazine articles. When *Casualties* was published I sent him a copy inscribed: *To Ralph from Lisa. I could never have done it without you.* I doubt if he understood. Whenever I get bogged down in whatever I'm writing I think of Ralph puffing his pipe and wearing his English corduroys and airing someone else's opinions and I find a good reason for going on.'

'How old are you?'

'Twenty-seven going on ninety.'

'So you've been on the loose for three years. You must have had lovers.'

'Yes. Like you.'

Greeve thought of all the forgotten prostitutes. 'I've forgotten them.'

'So have I.'

'Are we special?'

She raised her head and looked down at him. Her hair tickled him and her breasts spread against his chest and she was the most beautiful and desirable woman he had ever known.

'Alan, it will be a real kick in the gut if we're not special.'

He pulled her down and kissed her and held her tightly.

'Lisa, if we're not special, the rest of my life will be pretty damn pointless. It's too soon to talk about love. I haven't used the word in years and I don't want to use it lightly. Let's wait and see what happens.'

'I'll go with that. But promise you won't hurt me.'

He moved so he could see her face. 'Why should I hurt you?'

'I don't know why. But I keep getting hurt.'

'I wouldn't do that. I'd never do that.'

'I want to believe you.'

'Believe me. Trust me.'

'OK.' She yawned. 'I'd like to make love again, but I'd also like to go to sleep.'

'I'll put the light off.'

She was asleep before he got back into bed. He put his arms round her and she sighed and nestled against him.

He lay there in the darkness and marvelled at what had happened. It was eleven years since he had last made love to any woman apart from prostitutes, and then it had been Gilly, gentle and loving but sturdy rather than shapely. He had forgotten the intensity of passion, the way every word and gesture a woman made could be so important, the desire to please a woman and make her happy. He had forgotten so much. And maybe he'd never really understood. There had never been anyone like Lisa, never anyone who set him on fire like this.

Then he thought of Heward. Tomorrow was Wednesday. Wednesdays he phoned Heward.

Maybe tomorrow Heward would call him in for a briefing and he'd find himself with a contract to kill Lisa Castelle.

Over breakfast Greeve suggested they take a few days holiday. She looked doubtful.

'I have so much to do, Alan.'

'Any arrangements, any appointments?'

'Nothing definite.'

'So take a break. We'll get rid of one of the cars, go to Arles, find a *pension*, pretend we're married, have a look at Van Gogh country, drink the wine and eat bread and cheese and make love and get to know each other.'

'What about your friends, the people you were going to meet?'

'I'll spin them a story. It was an open invitation. If I tell them I'm on the track of an important painting they'll understand. I'll call them this afternoon.'

Lisa smiled. 'It's tempting. I haven't had a vacation since – since God knows when. Christmas, I think. And even then I had an article to write.'

'No writing. No research. No plans. We'll just do whatever we fancy doing.'

'Why do you want to pretend we're married?'

'If I use my name no one will be able to find you.'

'Good thinking, Batman.'

They kept Greeve's car and were in Arles by midday. They lunched in a café then went looking for a place to stay, settling on a small hotel a couple of miles out of the town. The room was on the north side of the old building, cool and airy, with a huge brass bed and creaking floorboards and a bathroom the size of a garage. They decided they ought to make sure the bed was the right length and width, something they could do only by stripping off and getting between the crisp white sheets and making love slowly for an hour. When Lisa was asleep Greeve dressed quietly and went in search of a phone.

'My name's Robert Redford. Mr Lomax, please.'

'I'm afraid you have a wrong number.'

'I'll wait until Bastille Day.'

'One moment, please.'

Heward came on. 'Hello, Sergeant.'

'You have something for me?'

'No. But I wanted a word, just to keep you up-to-date. The young lady you mentioned: we've been looking into things and there's a distinct possibility we may be doing business with her, possibly at short notice. Where are you?'

'Not local.'

'Perhaps we could have a word on Friday. We may have to meet. Call me.'

'OK.'

They visited the Roman theatre and amphitheatre and the ramparts and the various *musées*. The business community of Arles must have been cursing their predecessors for not preserving every last little reference to Vincent Van Gogh, the bar where he and Gauguin got drunk and his chair and his bed and so on. The Americans bombed Arles in 1944 and destroyed the house Van Gogh lived in while he was there in 1888.

They walked the countryside and tried to recognize the scenes Van Gogh had painted but they were too wrapped up in each other to have much time left for a dead painter.

It was like being on honeymoon, Greeve decided. They learned to wake up to each other and how to talk to each other and sorted out the little personal quirks everyone has and killed time until they could make love again. It was good and unlike anything he had ever experienced and although he avoided using the word love he knew he loved her and, by comparison, that he had never loved anyone else. This was a new sensation but he was old enough and experienced enough to recognize that he wasn't just blinded by lust.

They talked for hours. They would start a conversation over breakfast in the cramped little dining-room and continue it while they drove out into the country and walked along the edges of the fields and through the clumps of sun-dried pines, and finish it over wine and bread and soup somewhere and once they stopped talking just long enough to make love in the long grass behind a hedge.

The line from France was bad. Lacey closed his eyes and pressed the phone against his ear.

'Say again.'

'The subject was in Aix-en-Provence until yesterday morning, sir. She booked in under her own name a few days ago and apparently spent most of her time away from the hotel. She was alone until Monday the sixth. Then a man by the name of Alan Sinclair arrived saying he was expecting to meet her. They talked for an hour and a half over coffee. I don't know if they spent the night together, but they certainly had breakfast together. I picked her up as she left the hotel. She went off alone and wandered about for a long time and eventually went into a house on the Rue Fabrot. She was there about two hours. Then she went back to the hotel. Sinclair wasn't there. She spent the afternoon in her room then they went out to dinner and then spent the night together.'

'Who did she talk to in the Rue Fabrot?'

'The name on the door was S. Maupin.'

'What did this man Sinclair look like?'

'Male Caucasian. Mid-thirties. About six feet, one hundred and seventy pounds, clean-shaven, medium-length dark hair. Perhaps some kind of sportsman – he looked really fit, really hard. Unobtrusive: I mean, he had a knack of not attracting attention to himself. I couldn't get too close, but I think he spoke educated English.'

Lacey felt a prickle of alarm at the back of his neck.

'You didn't notice a scar on his right arm?'

'No, sir.'

'Grey eyes?'

'Grey-blue, I'd say, sir.'

'I need to see a photograph of this man.'

'I ran off some film.'

'Get it developed and wire me a good shot. All right, go on.'

'This morning she handed in her rented car and she and Sinclair went off together in his car. I lost them in traffic. They were heading west, towards Salon. That's where I am now, but I haven't managed to find them yet. Maybe they just passed through. They could have gone to Avignon or joined the N7 and be half-way to Paris by now. I need help, sir. It's a helluva job for one man.'

'Yes, yes, I know.' Lacey ran his hand through his cropped hair. 'I'll try to arrange some assistance. Keep looking. Keep me informed.'

He stared at the silent phone for a long time. The description fitted Greeve, but then Greeve was unremarkable and the description could have fitted thousands of men. Edwin Greasley wasn't capable of recognizing a genuine educated English accent. Greeve's attempts at losing his foul provincial snarl had been successful but an alert ear could pick out the failings.

But what if it were Greeve? What the hell was Greeve doing shacked up with Lisa Castelle? It seemed inconceivable that he would go anywhere near the daughter of a man he had excised, a woman he knew was under suspicion, a possible future contract. It just didn't hang together.

Lacey shook his head. No sense looking for trouble. Lisa Castelle was a very attractive young woman and there would be no shortage of men eager to get her into bed. The chances of the man in Aix-en-Provence being Greeve were remote.

· Nine ·

On the Friday morning Greeve suggested they move on to Avignon.

'Let's make it Nice, Alan.'

'Why Nice?'

She made the little face he'd learned to recognize as meaning, Don't be hurt.

'There's someone I need to talk to.'

'Important?'

'Yes.'

He didn't want her other life intruding on their idyll. As far as he was concerned they were the only people in the world.

She could see his hesitation and without prompting she came out with what he'd been wanting to know, the answers to the questions he had avoided asking in case she became suspicious.

'This is very secret, darling. I know I can trust you but you must promise not to say anything about it to anyone until after publication, or at least until I've found out who killed Dad.'

'Promise.'

'You've read Dad's book about Irangate. While he was researching it he thought he'd found a new connection and followed it for a long time but it turned out to be a completely different story. It's still about the sale of arms and missile guidance systems and materials for manufacturing nuclear weapons, things like that; it still involves important people; it's still about huge sums of money and barter and drugs and treachery and young American soldiers being killed by American weapons sold to America's enemies, but the cast list is different. Dad talked to me about it a couple of times and the last time I saw him he gave me a stack of notebooks and a draft of the first eight chapters of a book. He told me to put them in a safe place because he couldn't risk taking them with him. Then he flew off to Europe and three weeks later he was killed in Marseille.'

'You reckon he was killed because he was getting too near the truth?'

'Yes.'

How much of this did she believe? Or was it really true? He wanted to believe her. He didn't want her being an Iraqi recruit.

She read the doubt in his face.

'These things happen, Alan. Life is a lot dirtier than you can imagine. There are people, nice gentle, innocent people, who spend their time looking for forgotten paintings; but there are other people who spend their lives making huge sums of money out of arms and drugs and bribery and corruption and death.'

'Who are these people?'

'Dad identified six of them, five men and a woman. I've found three more. But these are just minions, serfs, soldiers, and one of them is dead. And, I must say, I may have to take some of those names off the list eventually, because it's desperately difficult to find proof. There was one other name, but even Dad was doubtful about him because he's a legitimate arms dealer. It's so hard to pin anyone down, so hard to get a straight answer. The fact that a man in Paris is a close associate of another man in Texas and meets him regularly is not exactly the kind of proof a court would accept.'

'And you believe it was these people who killed your father?'

'Of course.'

'Which countries are involved? As customers, I mean.'

'A lot of places in Africa; Africa seems to consume arms at an astonishing rate. Bosnia. Pakistan. Cambodia. The Middle East generally. There's no shortage of customers.'

'These people you've talked to – did they admit to being involved?'

'I didn't say I'd talked to all of them. That would be pushing my luck a bit too far. I've talked to people who know them or have had dealings with them. And I've talked to their competitors. The arms industry is huge and there are lots of people who do it perfectly legitimately and they hear things and get suspicious. These are my main sources of information.'

'The guy who was killed – Roth? – where did he fit in?'

'Dad called him a broker. He was a contact man. He brought the sellers and the buyers together.'

'So he could have given you a lot of information.'

'He could have, but he didn't. He'd talked to Dad and given him a few hints, mostly out of vanity, I think, but he wasn't about to risk his income and his life by providing details. All he was prepared to do for me was to confirm a few possibilities. I think the fact that he hoped to get inside my pants may have affected his judgement. But he was very nervous.'

'For good reason, obviously.'

'Yes. There's a very good chance he was killed because he talked to me and that's a lot to have on your conscience.'

Greeve's mind was racing. 'They, whoever they are,

must have been very close to either you or Roth to have been in a position to kill him within an hour or two of your meeting.'

'The meeting was arranged weeks earlier. I called him from San Francisco and said I'd be in Europe and could I meet him and he suggested Paris. We arranged the date and the time and the restaurant. I was a bit surprised when he took me back to his apartment. He'd been drinking a lot and he was in a good mood and I hoped he'd open up a bit more but he didn't get the chance.'

'So who do you want to see in Nice?'

'Dad quoted a name. Georges Ferrat. A retired pilot who is supposed to have flown arms shipments around the world for the group. If I can get him to confirm he made a particular flight from Marseille to Iraq in 1986 I'll have an important piece of the jigsaw; it'll be confirmation of a deal I know was tied up in Marseille a few weeks earlier. If we go to Nice, would you want to stay with your friends?'

'They've left.' Greeve glanced at his watch. 'They're probably in the air right now. Anyway, I wouldn't have wanted to share our time with them. I'd rather we were alone together as much as possible.'

'So it's back to the *Guide Michelin?*'

'Looks like it.'

'I'll call Georges Ferrat and see if he'll talk to me.'

Greeve was packing when Lisa came into the room, her face bright with excitement.

'It's fixed. I'm meeting him at his apartment in Nice at seven o'clock tonight. Maybe this will be the break I need.'

Rossi took the call.

'It's Georges Ferrat, Boss, calling from Nice.'

Carver frowned. 'What the hell is that lush calling about?'

'Didn't say, Boss.'

Carver took the receiver. *'Georges, mon ami! Comment ça va?'*

He listened carefully, the frown gathering between the heavy brows, the scowl deepening at the corners of the thick lips.

'Georges, when she arrives, keep her talking as long as you can. Don't do anything else. What?' He listened again. 'You tell her nothing, of course. Deny everything.'

He slammed the phone down and cursed angrily. Rossi stood by, keeping silent. Carver in a bad mood had to be handled very gently.

The Texan picked up the phone again and punched out a number. 'Mr Lacey, please. Tell him it's Jack Houston from CIA Headquarters, Langley.'

He waited, knowing the phone was secure.

'Lacey.'

'I've had a call from that drunk Georges Ferrat in Nice. He says Lisa Castelle wants to talk to him. He's fixed a time – eight o'clock tonight, at his apartment. I don't like this, my friend. If she's on to Ferrat it means she's getting too damn close. But at least now we know where she is. I want you to put out a contract on her immediately.'

'These things take time to arrange. But I have one of our official people in the area. I can use him to get a fix on her and follow up with a contract.'

'Do that, my friend. Do it now.'

Lacey replaced the phone and glanced at his watch. Greasley would be calling in with what would no doubt be another negative situation report in less than half an hour. There was plenty of time to set it all up, get him into position outside Georges Ferrat's apartment; Greasley was a distasteful little peasant, but he was the best solo tail in the department. The Lisa Castelle contract would have to go to Ryder, who was good but inexperienced.

Greeve had to be checked out first.

* * *

Nice is expensive, even in September. They took a room at a small hotel, again using Greeve's fake name, then rode a taxi into the town centre and separated to do some shopping. Greeve bought what he needed then went to the café where they had arranged to meet and ordered coffee and cognac and sat deep in thought.

Before, during and especially after the Gulf War it had been difficult for Saddam Hussein to buy the huge quantities of weaponry he needed. Maybe Lisa Castelle's story could be looked at from an entirely different point of view. Maybe her story about investigating illegal arms shipments was a neat cover for buying armaments for Iraq.

Greeve still refused to believe it. He was aware that his reaction was unprofessional and subjective and that if Lisa Castelle had been an ugly middle-aged woman with bad breath he would have believed the worst. He knew he was infatuated by her and that his judgement was necessarily suspect.

And even if it were true, even if Lisa were everything Heward thought she was, he might still not do anything about it. He couldn't really see himself putting a gun to Lisa's head and squeezing the trigger.

He loved her. It wasn't just infatuation or lust or the obsession of a man bemused by the intensity of his own emotions. He actually loved her, and he now understood, also, that he had never really loved anyone else. With Gilly and Linda it had been affection, fondness, a warm back on a cold night, nothing more. There had never been anything like this overwhelming sense of completeness and togetherness and total involvement. There had never been this mutual fire and excitement and passion and almost telepathic understanding. It was still almost

unbelievable that it should have happened with someone
so beautiful, so exquisite.

Just this morning, in the hotel room near Arles, he had
wakened first and had lain for a long time looking at her,
marvelling at her tumbled beauty, the perfection of her
skin, the curve of the dark lashes, the full, soft lips. She
had been lying on her back, one arm behind her head,
naked under the sheet, and he had lifted the cotton away
gently and caught her warm musk and felt the reaction at
the sight of her breasts, one rounded and perfect, the
other pulled taut by the angle of her arm, the nipples soft
and smooth. It had been more than he could bear. He had
moved carefully down the bed until he could reach her
breasts with his mouth and she had come slowly awake
and without saying anything had begun to stroke his
back. When he threw the sheet aside and ran his fingers
down her belly to the dark triangle she had sighed and
spread her legs wide, uninhibited, luxuriating in the
moment. She had let him do whatever he wanted, her
eyes closed, a little smile on her face, doing nothing to
rouse him, prolonging the pleasure and, when he slipped
into her, she had lain there with her arms outstretched,
knowing there was nothing she need do to make the
event better, knowing he wanted it this way. When they
climaxed she still said nothing, still didn't open her eyes.
Instead, she had rolled over and snuggled into his side
and gone back to sleep, one tawny thigh across his hips,
one hand caressing his chest. He had lain there, not
wanting to sleep, not wanting to lose a moment of this
time, loving her intensely.

He saw her walking along the street towards the café,
the sun making a halo of her hair, her graceful legs
silhouetted through the thin cotton of her dress, her head
high and her face alight with happiness, and decided it
was time to tell her. It was eleven years since he had used

the word love and he had been putting off the moment, fearful that she might draw back from such a commitment, afraid that he might scare her off in some way.

She saw him and smiled and threaded her way between the tables to join him. He ordered coffee and cognac; she was learning to like the stuff.

'I was thinking, maybe I should come along with you tonight.'

'I told Ferrat I'd have you with me. I hope you don't mind.'

'No problem.'

'Well, we have time on our hands. What'll we do?'

Their eyes met. Greeve leant closer and whispered, 'How would it be if we went back to the hotel and took a shower together and then you could lie on your tummy on the bed and I'll start at your feet and work my way slowly up the backs of your legs till I reach your gorgeous little backside and the small of your back and I'll go right up your spine to that little bit at the top that makes you giggle. Then when you can't take it any more I'll turn you over and start all over again until you're begging for it and then I'll do it some more.'

'More detail. Give me more detail.'

'Your feet are beautiful. I love them. And the skin behind your knees is so smooth and perfect and the insides of your thighs are the most erotic I've ever had the privilege of kissing and that dark little triangle at the top is a delight and I love the way you cup your breast and offer me the nipple. I want you to do that for me. And I want you to flavour your nipples with your juices for me to lick off....'

She tossed the last of her brandy down her throat and got to her feet.

'Let's go, lover.'

'I haven't finished.'

'I almost have. Let's go.'

While they were standing on the pavement waving at taxis he put his arm round her shoulder and kissed the top of her head.

'Love you.'

'Is this just a hard-on talking or do you mean it?'

'I mean it.'

'You choose the oddest times to say the important things. I love you, too.'

'Nice arrangement.'

'You can never get a taxi when you want one in a hurry.'

Lacey sat at his desk staring in shock at the copy of the photograph Greasley had wired from France. It showed Lisa Castelle and John Greeve getting into a taxi outside a hotel. The woman was certainly beautiful – stunningly so, in that red dress – and there was something about the way they were smiling at each other which suggested their relationship was not casual.

For God's sake, how? How had these two come together, Hugo Castelle's daughter and the man who had killed Hugo Castelle? How long had they been friends? How much did they know about each other? What had they told each other? What was the connection?

But did it matter? Simply by being together they had signed their own death warrants. They would soon be dead, and that would be an end to the problem. But quickly, quickly, before things became even more complicated.

Pity about Greeve. He'd been the best hatchet man Lacey had ever employed.

Should he tell Carver? How would the millionaire react? As he always did, no doubt: *I pay you big money, Lacey. For that money I want efficiency, I want speed, I want loyalty. I want to give you my problems and forget about them. I do not want you coming to me with problems. Problems are your problem.* It seemed better to keep quiet about Greeve. Carver had no idea who carried out the contracts; all he was interested in was the results.

It was important that Lacey maintain the impression Carver had, that for his money he received a competent and professional service.

Besides, Ryder was cheaper than Greeve.

Lacey looked at his watch again. Ryder always called early in his two-hour, Friday-afternoon time slot....

'It's Michael Norris, sir.'

Ryder's instructions were to call in using a name with successive initial capitals.

'I'll take it.... Hello, Lieutenant.'

'You have something for me, sir?'

'Yes, I have. We'd better meet. It's a rush job, so we'll skip the usual routine. I'll book a room for you at the Russell under the name of Henry Stirling, 11 Skues Crescent, Carlisle. Be there at nine tonight. Leave the door open. And be ready to travel.'

'Foreign?'

'Yes. France.'

'For how long, sir?'

'Just a few days.'

'Very good, sir.'

Greeve could learn a lot from Ryder about how to address a superior, Lacey thought sourly. But it was too late for Greeve to learn.

· Ten ·

Georges Ferrat lived in a second-floor apartment off the Boulevard de Cimiez. The door was opened by a thin woman with a lot of curly black hair. Lisa identified herself and they were ushered into an untidy hallway smelling of garlic and strong tobacco.

'Through here. He's waiting for you. Don't be put off if he's in a bad mood.' Her French was fluent but not her native tongue. She left them to find their own way.

Greeve pushed open the door and at first thought the big room was empty. Then he saw a pair of bare feet protruding from the end of a couch and went closer and saw a long thin man stretched out, his cropped white head on a cushion, his eyes closed, a Gitane burning between thin lips. He was unshaven and the vest and jeans he was wearing looked none too clean.

'M'sieu Ferrat?'

The tortoise eyes opened slowly. The pilot stared at them for a long moment then eased himself stiffly into a sitting position, reached for a glass on the dusty coffee-table and poured something down his throat. He seemed to shiver then come alive. He waved a hand at the furniture.

'Sit down. Jeanne!'

The woman appeared. In the dim light of the hallway

she had looked reasonably attractive, but here in the sitting-room her age showed and it was obvious that her hair had been dyed.

'Drinks for our guests. And for me.'

'You've had enough, Georges.'

He tapped his forefinger several times on the coffee-table; the sound seemed menacingly loud. The woman poured three glasses of cognac and passed them around then went out again.

'So: it is Miss Castelle, isn't it? Come to pick my addled brain and try to get me to condemn myself.' His voice was educated but slurred, his English only slightly accented. His fingers were stained with nicotine. 'And this gentleman is ...?'

'Alan Sinclair. My companion.'

Ferrat looked at Greeve. The long, bony face seemed to be set in a permanent sneer. He gave a shrug of the shoulders which apparently consigned Greeve to the outer reaches of irrelevance. Then he glanced at his watch and frowned.

'You are early. We agreed eight o'clock.'

'Seven.' Lisa opened her notebook. 'I wrote it down.'

'I said eight!' Ferrat's anger seemed out of proportion to the offence. 'Eight o'clock! Definitely!'

Greeve watched Lisa use her charm. 'Is it important, Georges? We could come back later if you want.'

He shrugged and made a face, clearly unable to maintain his annoyance under the influence of her beauty. 'It's nothing. Of no importance. But I have nothing of interest to say to you, mademoiselle.'

'You were a pilot....'

'I am still a pilot. A little difficulty about my licence. A little disagreement about drinking.'

'Did you have your own plane?'

'But of course.'

'Do you still have it?'

He fitted another Gitane between the thin lips. 'I sold it. It needed a lot of work. I couldn't afford it.'

'Did you make a trip from Marseille to Iraq in 1986?'

'Perhaps. I don't remember. I flew everywhere.' He emptied the glass and immediately rose and steadied himself and went to the sideboard to bring back the bottle.

'Do you still have your records, the log book and so on?'

'Unfortunately, no. They were lost. But all flights are notified and you can consult the appropriate authority, if you have a month or two to spare.'

'Will these records show you were carrying arms to Iraq?'

'No.' He looked at Lisa with contempt. 'Are you really as foolish as you sound, mademoiselle?'

'M'sieu Ferrat, I'm not interested in you; I've no wish to get you into difficulties. No one knows I'm here; no one will ever know you've talked to me. All I need to know is, did you fly a consignment of arms to Iraq on October 16, 1986? If you can confirm that flight I'll leave immediately and you'll never hear from me again.'

'I never flew such a cargo. Machinery, medical supplies, yes; but not arms. Ever.'

'I'm prepared to pay for the information.'

'How much?'

Greeve was not surprised at Ferrat's sudden change of tone. The brandy was cheap and harsh and there were two rectangles of lighter colour on the walls which suggested the pilot must have had to sell paintings. There was less furniture in the room than might have been expected. A co-axial cable appeared from a socket in the wall but there was no television. Georges Ferrat was in financial trouble.

A handful of notes changed hands.

'Tell me about the flight, M'sieu Ferrat.'

'Put the notebook away, mademoiselle.'

'But....'

'You will no doubt write up your notes later. But if you do that I can deny you were ever here, that you are writing fiction.'

Greeve watched closely. The Frenchman's eyes flicked to his watch yet again.

'All right. Is the date correct?'

'Yes.'

'You flew from Marseille to Baghdad?'

'Yes.'

'What was in the cargo?'

He shrugged. 'Wooden boxes, metal boxes. All marked as medical equipment. I don't know more than that. And I shall deny all knowledge of arms, if necessary.'

'Who delivered the arms to you?'

'You did not pay for that information, mademoiselle.'

Lisa held up a photograph. 'Was it this man?'

Ferrat shrugged. 'I forget.'

Another photograph. 'This man?'

His eyes flickered. 'Who knows?'

Greeve tried to see the photographs but failed.

'Was there any difficulty about getting the flight through Customs?'

'Of course not.' Ferrat seemed to find the idea amusing.

'These men you don't remember: were they French? Or was one of them perhaps American?'

'We did not talk much.'

'You would have known.'

'Perhaps.'

Lisa sighed impatiently. 'Was there a return cargo?'

'Yes.'

'Drugs.' She made it should like a statement rather than a query.

Ferrat shook his head. 'Coffee.'

'From Iraq?'

'Why not?'

Lisa paused. 'Hugo Castelle was shot dead in a hotel room in Marseille about a year ago. You met him some time before that.'

'I don't remember.'

'The papers said he was involved in drugs in some way and that the killing was drugs-related. Do you think that was true?'

Ferrat shrugged. 'Who knows?'

'Perhaps he was killed because he was investigating illegal arms shipments.'

'Perhaps.'

'If he was killed for that reason, who might have wanted him dead?'

'Many people. It's a big industry, big money, very dangerous for everyone. You should be careful, mam'selle.'

'Do you know who killed my father?'

'No.'

'Who might know?'

'The man who killed him.'

'Who might know that man?'

Ferrat shrugged again. Ash from the cigarette fell down the front of the vest.

Greeve rose. 'Time to go, Lisa.'

'What?' She looked at him in astonishment.

'We have to meet Phillipe in half an hour.' He held her eyes, willing her to play along with the fiction, and she sensed his urgency.

'I'd forgotten.' She got to her feet. 'Thank you, Georges.'

'Don't go yet, my friends.' Ferrat tried to struggle off the couch but failed. 'Stay. Have another drink. Coffee. Jeanne!'

'Perhaps another time, m'sieu,' Greeve said, his hand gripping Lisa's arm and setting her in motion towards the door. 'Thank you.'

Lisa resisted. 'One last question. Georges, are you still in touch with Carver?'

Drunk as he was, the Frenchman almost managed to disguise his reaction. He shrugged elaborately and looked blank.

'Mam'selle?'

On the stairs Lisa turned to Greeve, annoyed. 'I wasn't finished. What's wrong?'

'I'm not sure, but I'm damn sure something is. Keep moving. When we reach the street, don't stand around: get into the car as quickly as possible but without making a scene of it.'

Greeve drove north up the boulevard then detoured round several blocks before returning to park in a row of cars on the opposite side from Ferrat's apartment and a hundred yards away.

'Tell me if you recognize anyone.'

'Who do you expect?'

'I don't know.' Greeve was trying to see into cars. 'But there's something wrong. It made no sense, a drunk lying there doing nothing then getting pissed off about the time we arrived. And he checked his watch another three times while we were there. I got the impression he was expecting someone to arrive. Maybe he'd called someone to say you were meeting him but screwed up the time. Just keep your eyes open.'

They watched the street for a while. There were few people about.

Lisa pointed. 'Look!'

Greeve had already seen Georges Ferrat appear at the big door and look around. Immediately, a car door opened and a man climbed out and crossed the road.

They spoke together for a minute, Ferrat spreading his hands helplessly, the other man clearly angry. Greeve noted the stranger's appearance carefully: about 5'6", by comparison with the pilot; mid-forties, wiry, sandy hair balding, possibly a moustache. He looked English.

The conference ended. The stranger got into his car and drove off. Ferrat made an expressive gesture and went back inside.

'Recognize him?'

Lisa shook her head. 'Never seen him before.' She looked frightened.

Greeve started the engine and pulled out and followed the distant car. A left, a right, another left, another right ... and then the other car had vanished. More accurately, the streets were full of small Renaults. Greeve cruised for a few minutes then gave up and headed back towards their hotel.

'You didn't get much out of Georges Ferrat.'

'I got the confirmation I needed of the flight; he recognized one of the photographs; he confirmed the return cargo was drugs.'

'He said coffee.'

'They pack the drugs in ground coffee to disguise the smell, so the sniffer dogs won't find them.'

'Who were the men in the photographs?'

'They're people Dad tracked down. He took the pictures. Long-range, with a small camera, but he knew what he was doing.'

'Who's the Carver you mentioned?'

'That was a long shot. Eugene Carver runs an apparently legitimate arms company in Texas. But his name was among Dad's notes, with a big question mark beside it. Georges Ferrat flew some legitimate deliveries for Carver.'

'Are you any further forward?'

Lisa sat low in her seat, her face downcast. 'Not really. It's very difficult to get anything new. It's very difficult to get to the sources. Everything's secondhand. I don't have Dad's contacts or his nose for a lead or his brass neck or his courage.'

'You do pretty well. When it comes to courage, I mean.'

'You're wrong. I'm frightened. I've a bad feeling I may have got myself into something pretty nasty and that the people who killed Dad are now closing in on me.'

'I'm glad you said it and not me. I've had that feeling for some time, but I guessed that if I suggested you give up it would just make you more determined.'

'I didn't say I've given up. It's just.... I don't know. I'll have to think about it. Still love me?'

'Yes.'

She was silent for a long moment.

'Right now, that's more important than anything else. Let's go to bed and not make love.'

'Is that possible?'

'Let's try. I just want to be safe and warm and reassured. Especially safe.'

Neither of them saw the small Renault which drove slowly past as they walked into the hotel.

Carver listened carefully to what Ferrat had to say.

'You did your best, my friend. Thank you.'

He replaced the phone and smashed his fist down on the coffee-table.

'Useless French lush! Jesus, why do I have to put up with drunken assholes who can't even tell the fucking time correctly?'

He picked up the phone again and stabbed at the buttons. Lacey had gone home for the evening. He dialled a second number.

'Hello?'

'Our lady friend in France has my name. I want her contract terminated immediately.'

'It's in hand.'

'I want it done now, my friend. Right now. And the guy with her. His name's Alan Sinclair.'

'We're already on to them. I've just had a call from my man in Nice. He managed to pick them up, despite some confusion over the timing of their meet with Georges Ferrat....'

'I know about that. My apologies.'

'No harm done. My man knows where they're staying. I'm just leaving to meet my representative and brief him.'

'Don't let me keep you.'

Angela was putting the dinner dishes in the dishwasher in the farmhouse-style kitchen. Lacey took the car keys from the row of hooks.

'I have to go out for an hour or so. Business.'

'What's her name?'

'Let's not start that again, Angela. You know the work I do: we don't keep normal business hours.'

She turned her back on him and rattled the dishes noisily and he sighed. It was going to be another of those nights. She dispensed sex in small quantities, grudgingly, seemingly determined to make sure he knew she did not enjoy the experience, then became violently jealous when she thought he was getting it elsewhere. Not for the first time Lacey indulged himself in the daydream of a life without Angela. And the children.

Ryder's attitude to Lacey was much more respectful than Greeve's. Ryder knew how to behave. Ryder was from the same social class as Lacey and understood the way things should be done. Ryder had been to a good public school before following his father into the Army and might well have advanced to a higher rank than lieutenant if it hadn't been for the ruthless streak which had left two Argentinian POWs dead in the closing days of the Falklands conflict. The matter had been suppressed. Lacey had vetted the man carefully, identified the stunted emotional development, the essential iciness required of a good assassin, and had arranged a meeting. Ryder had taken longer than Greeve to make up his mind, and the discussion over payment had been protracted, but Ryder was still on a lower scale than Greeve. The lieutenant had no idea Greeve existed. His two contracts so far had not been difficult but he had handled them with military precision and Lacey had high hopes for him.

'Good evening, Lieutenant.'

'Good evening, sir. Drink?' There was a half-bottle of Grouse and two glasses on the bedside cabinet.

'Thank you. A little water.'

Ryder looked fit. He was a solidly built man, a little under six feet, square-faced, clean-shaven. His belly was flat, his thigh muscles evident under the tailored slacks. The tightly waved yellow hair was trimmed into a short-back-and-sides, parted on the left. The grey eyes were steady and suggested considerable self-confidence, and the slightly misshapen nose, the result of a boxing injury, saved him from being just a little too handsome. He had been taught to inspire confidence in his men by being confident of his own abilities and the attitude still showed. He spoke well, his voice clipped, the enunciation correct and curt.

Lacey switched on the television and turned the sound a little higher then took the chair; Ryder sat on the bed. Lacey drew a sheaf of papers from an inside pocket and sorted through them.

'We have an urgent situation, Lieutenant.' He passed the younger man a photograph. 'This is a KGB man by the name of Godunov, but you'd be hard put to recognize him as anything but an Englishman. At the moment he's using the name Alan Sinclair. That photograph is several years old but he hasn't changed much. You don't need to know the full background, of course; I'll simply say he's a very clever and resourceful operative who has a number of high-grade successes to his credit, most of them against us. At the moment he is working with one of his colleagues, a woman using the name Lisa Castelle. She may or may not be his wife. They certainly co-habit. This is the woman.'

Ryder studied the second photograph. 'Quite a looker.' He paused, frowning. 'I think I've seen her somewhere.'

Lacey was ready for the possibility that Ryder had read Lisa Castelle's book.

'Probably on the back of a book jacket. She operates under the cover of being an American journalist and writer. She wrote a book about Vietnam veterans.'

'I remember. I read it.'

'She's very good, highly skilled. She was actually born in the States. Her father was a deep-cover KGB agent for many years. We took him out in Marseille about a year ago. We let Godunov and his woman run for a while, half-thinking the changes in Moscow might mean they would be recalled, but they're still hard at work. Obviously, I can't tell you what they're doing, but if they succeed it will cost us millions to repair the damage. I should add that these people are dangerous. We know they have both killed in the line of duty. The man is particularly lethal. You'll have to be very careful.'

'Where are they?'

'At the moment, in a hotel in Nice. They've been moving about quite a lot, under a variety of names, so you'll have to zero in on them as quickly as possible. We have a tail on them, so if they've moved on just contact me and I'll let you know where they've gone. Don't waste time on elaborate plans: get the job done and get out. Every day that passes causes us more trouble. Right – the details: passport, papers, weapon, travel.'

Lacey glanced at Ryder. There was no suggestion of doubt or hesitation in the man's face. Was he a match for Greeve? Why shouldn't he be? Greeve wasn't expecting trouble, and he had no experience of being a target.

· **Eleven** ·

'I'm frightened, Alan.'

Greeve had been under the impression Lisa was asleep. They had returned to the hotel, had a drink in the bar and gone to bed early. When he slid in beside her she had been lying with her back to him and he had chosen not to disturb her. Her words came as a surprise.

She turned and put her arm over his chest and rested her head on his shoulder.

'When I started on this thing I was angry – outraged – full of piss and vinegar. I was determined to find the man who had killed Dad and identify him and see him in court. And then, of course, write a book about it and win another award and earn lots of money and really fix my reputation as a crusading investigative writer. I'm beginning to realize just how naive I was.'

Greeve stroked her hair. 'Not naive. It's not naive to be beaten by an unknown force much stronger than yourself.'

'Do you think I'm in danger?'

It was a time to be honest. 'Yes, I think you are. I think Georges Ferrat reported to someone that you wanted to talk to him and was told to go ahead with the interview to allow someone else to get a fix on you. But there was a cock-up over the timing and the man we saw missed you.

I'm not sure about Bodo Roth, but it seems too much of a coincidence, his being killed while you were with him. Maybe it was a warning. Yes, I think you're in danger. If they decide you're getting too near to the truth they may take action against you. That man we saw tonight may be the first move.'

'Would it be chickening out to stop now and give up and go home?'

'It would be very sensible.'

'Do you think that would be the end of it? Would they know I'd stopped? Would they leave me alone?'

Greeve frowned into the darkness. 'How would they know you'd stopped? How would they know you'd given up?'

'They wouldn't.'

Minutes passed. Greeve broke the silence.

'What do we know? You've talked to a lot of people. You may not have talked to anyone important, but the chances are the word will have reached the people who matter that you're working on the story. They'll be nervous. They won't like the idea of a journalist asking questions about them. To them, that means you're going to write about them. For all you know, you may be nearer the truth than you realize. Ferrat said these people are dangerous and I think we can accept that.'

'They killed Dad.'

No, I did that. You're getting two different stories mixed up.

He could feel the warmth of her thigh against his and the slight movement of her fingers on his chest; he wanted to turn to her and embrace her but he knew what would happen if he did and this wasn't the time. Her breath tickled his skin and he could smell the scent of her shampoo. He moved his arm, encircling her, and ran his hand down over the small of her back to the firm curve of her waist.

'Lisa, we don't know who else they've killed. Big money, high stakes, ruthless people. I don't think they'd hesitate to kill a potentially dangerous journalist who might be getting too close to them, no matter how young and lovely she is.'

She moved and he sensed her looking down at him in the darkness. Her voice held shock.

'Alan, they might kill you, too! They almost certainly would, just because you're with me. They'll assume we're working together and they'd have to kill you as well.'

'That would make sense.' Greeve had already considered the possibility.

'I can't let that happen, Alan. We … we'll have to separate.'

'Too late now. Much better if we vanished.'

'Before they find us.'

'They may already have found us.'

'But we avoided that man tonight.'

'Was he alone? Was there another car? Did they already know where we're staying?'

'Christ!' Lisa sat up and he saw her silhouetted against the curtained window. She spoke in a tense whisper. 'My God, Alan, they could be outside the door right now!'

Her fear communicated itself to Greeve and suddenly he felt the need for a gun. Preferably an automatic with thirty rounds in the mag.

'Take it easy, darling. Lie down. Let's not get in a panic. We'll leave first thing in the morning, change cars, find ourselves somewhere else to stay.'

'And then what?'

'Then we'll pause and consider.'

Where could he get a gun? Marseille, surely. Or there was the handgun he had left buried on the hillside in Switzerland after the Playboy contract. But Marseille might be quicker.

He rose and went to the window and moved the curtain

gently aside and studied the darkened street for a long time. An occasional car passed. A couple walked down the hill with their arms round each other, their laughter just audible. It was hard to tell if there were anyone sitting in the cars parked along the side of the road. If he himself had been contracted to hit someone in this hotel, how would he....

'Alan!'

'What?'

'The corridor!'

He crossed silently to the door and listened. Footsteps faded, a door was opened and closed. Silence.

'It's OK.'

He slid back into bed and knew immediately that it would be impossible to sleep.

'Go to sleep, Lisa. I'll stay awake. We'll move out first thing in the morning.'

'Where to?'

'I'll have to think about that.'

'I won't be able to sleep.'

'Try.'

She did sleep, eventually. Greeve lay awake, listening to every sound in the street, every passing car, every creak or footstep in the corridor, every flushed toilet, every indistinct murmur of voices.

Which was illogical, he decided, several times. If he had wanted to carry out a hit in a hotel he wouldn't do it in the middle of the night, when every moving figure, every footstep and creaking floorboard arouses suspicion; much better to do it late in the evening, when there are still people moving innocently around and the target can be observed going to his room. Follow him closely, make sure the corridor is empty, put a couple of quiet ones into the back of his head just as he's entering his room then pull the door shut on the body and walk casually away with an eight-hour head start.

Where could he and Lisa run to?

The answer to that was – nowhere.

If someone really wants to kill you and there's money available then there's really nowhere to hide. It may take longer, but short of government protection they will get you eventually.

The only other possibility is a complete change of identity: new name, new face, new location, a life in hiding. For that, again, you need government backing or a large private fortune.

The only alternative was to take out the enemy first. And he had no idea who the enemy was.

The only thing he knew for sure was that whatever happened to Lisa would happen to him too. There was no possibility of his abandoning her for the sake of his own safety.

He badly wanted a cigarette.

They left the hotel a little after seven the following morning, much to the annoyance of the night porter they found asleep in the lounge. Greeve apologized for the trouble they were causing and tipped generously.

'We have to be in Paris as quickly as possible. It's an emergency.'

The night porter shrugged to indicate his complete indifference to their private circumstances and left them to carry their own luggage. Greeve walked out into the morning sunlight feeling unpleasantly exposed, his eyes flicking from car to car, window to doorway to corner. Nothing happened. They threw their cases into the boot and got in and Greeve accelerated away.

'Paris? Why Paris?'

'We're not going to Paris. But if anyone asks the porter

where we've gone they might be sent off in the wrong direction. Watch for any car that looks like it's following us.'

'I don't see anything.'

They lost time searching for the car rental agency and then it was still closed. Impatient, Greeve carried on.

'We'll swop cars later. Go on watching for anyone tailing us.'

'There are dozens of cars. Hundreds.'

'Do your best.'

He drove fast, following the A8 to Aix then turning north on the A51 as far as Sisteron then taking to the side roads, still with no specific destination in mind. There was no evidence of a tail either behind or ahead. By mid-morning they were travelling on narrow roads deep in the hills and Lisa had recovered her self-confidence.

'Do you think we could stop and get some breakfast now? I'm starving.'

'Sounds like a good idea. Next village.'

'Do we have a plan, or are we just going to drive madly around France for the rest of our lives?'

'We'll find somewhere to stay for a few days while we decide what to do. I think what we have to do is try to work out who the enemy is and take it from there. What was the name your father mentioned, the one with the question mark against it?'

'Carver. Carver Arms and Systems of Texas.'

'What proof do you have that they might be involved?'

'Dad's notes, and one sentence in his draft typescript.'

'What did he say?'

'Something like: *It was only after my visit to Aix-en-Provence and my meeting with the dark woman that I began to have my suspicions about Carver Arms.*'

'The dark woman?'

'A woman called Simone Maupin. She was the woman I

talked to that day in Aix, the day you had your evil way with me. Dad didn't name her in the draft; he'd promised he wouldn't. But her name and address were in his notebooks.'

Greeve slowed for a fork in the road and went left because the surface looked better that way.

'Where does she fit into the picture?'

'Her husband was involved in illegal arms running. He was pulled out of the harbour at Trieste about eighteen months ago. Simone Maupin is very bitter. She reckons he was killed because he was asking for more money, and she feels guilty because she put him up to it.'

'Did she ever talk to the police about this?'

Lisa shook her head. 'She was questioned, of course, but she didn't tell them anything. That would have been dangerous, she said. Besides, there was a fairly generous handout from an unnamed source as compensation for the loss of her husband.'

'Did she mention Carver Arms?'

'To Dad, yes. Not to me. I got the impression she'd been instructed to keep her mouth shut. It was funny: she seemed to sympathize with me because Dad had been killed, just as her husband was, but at the same time she didn't want to say too much. Bribed and scared: a pretty lethal combination. She was nervous, couldn't get me out of the house fast enough.'

'Have you done any research on Carver Arms?'

'Some. Superficial. And Dad had done a little. I didn't want to waste too much time on that angle until I was sure I was on the right track. When you're researching a book, the biggest problem is time. You daren't waste effort on anything irrelevant.'

'Could we go through your notes? There might be something we could work on.'

She looked at him for a long moment. 'Perhaps later.'

Greeve swore silently. He had given her a false name, a false history, a false profession; he had forced an introduction by telling her a pack of lies; he had killed her father. It seemed unreasonable to complain that she still didn't trust him.

'Sorry. I take that back. It might be better if you didn't show me your notes. Anything rather than having you distrust me. I want to help, but being in love with you and having you love me is more important than anything else and I'm prepared to dump anything that might jeopardize that.'

'Maybe you've read my notes already.'

'No, I haven't.' He had been tempted to but something had prevented him, some idea of honesty or honour.

'You couldn't anyway, unless you read shorthand. And not just straightforward shorthand, but shorthand full of abbreviations and code words and so on.'

'I don't read shorthand.'

Lisa stared out at the wooded hillsides for a long time. 'I'm sorry, Alan. You didn't deserve that. I'm tired and frightened and I'm getting nowhere with this matter and I haven't found Dad's killer and I'm getting scared to trust anyone. You were just caught in the crossfire. Yes, we'll go through my notes and I'll be grateful for anything you can contribute.'

About eight miles behind them, Edwin Greasley steered the Renault with one knee while he rolled a cigarette from a crumpled half-ounce packet of Old Holborn. On the passenger seat a small black box hummed quietly, the nose rising and falling, sometimes changing from a buzz to a series of clicks and back again. The signal from the transmitter he had placed in one of the rear wheel arches of Sinclair's car was affected by the hills, but it told him the Peugeot was still ahead and moving at a steady speed.

The Michelin road map showed a village and a junction a few miles further on. He hoped Castelle and Sinclair would stop; after a restless night in the cheap hotel round the corner from where they had been staying, Greasley had been wakened when the slow click of the tracker had changed to a sudden buzz, forcing him to leave without breakfast, and he was now seriously hungry. His usual stock of fruit and nut chocolate was exhausted and there was just the one can of diet Coke left and his ulcer was showing signs of playing up. He needed a proper meal.

He got the needle-thin cigarette going and touched the redial button on the mobile; when Mrs Martin answered he asked to be put through to Lacey.

'Yes, Edwin?'

'They're still moving, sir, still heading generally north, possible destination Grenoble.'

'Thank you, Edwin. Keep in touch. If they stop, let me know immediately.'

'Yessir.'

Ryder called Lacey from the airport at Marseille. Lacey told him to rent a car and head for Grenoble.

The village was small and rather self-consciously quaint. They followed the smell of coffee and fresh bread to a café and while they ate Greeve asked the plump young woman if she knew of any holiday cottages available to rent in the neighbourhood. The plump young woman went to the kitchen to consult her father. Her father shouted upstairs to his wife. His wife shouted back. The young woman returned. It wasn't certain, remember, but madame at the farm had said something about a cancellation.

Would mademoiselle be so kind as to phone on their behalf? But certainly.

Yes, the cottage was available, from noon onwards for one week, this being Saturday. Madame would await their arrival at the farm. Follow the main road west for two kilometres, to where the bridge crossed the river, then take the first farm road on the left.

Merci, mademoiselle.

Money changed hands.

Ah, merci, m'sieu.

Madame was as neat and tidy as the small farm was ramshackle and her accent was almost incomprehensible. Greeve and Lisa exchanged doubtful glances; a diplomatic retreat might be called for if the cottage turned out to be in the same condition as the outbuildings. Madame climbed into the back seat of the car and directed Greeve to follow a grass track downhill through the trees towards the shallow river splashing over white stones. The cottage appeared suddenly; it was stone, single-storey, the roof red-tiled, and looked as if it had been baking in the sun for several hundred years.

Greeve parked on the grass near the front door and they all went inside. There were two rooms and a bathroom and everything was spotlessly clean. The furniture was dark and heavy, the pictures on the walls depressing, but the electric cooker and fridge were almost new and there was an electric shower above the gigantic cast-iron bath with its claw feet.

Greeve paid for the week and madame set off to walk back to the farm. Lisa explored the kitchen-sitting room, opening cupboards and drawers, examining the row of books on top of the polished chest of drawers.

'I love it! My God, Alan, have you ever seen anything like it? It's like living a hundred years in the past, except for the fridge and so on.'

Or in my house when I was young, Greeve thought, but

he kept silent about that. Besides, his house had never been this clean.

'We'd better get in some food and wine. Can you cook, Lisa?'

'I can open cans with the best of them. I can defrost a TV dinner. How about you?'

'Never had the chance to learn, really. We'll manage. Lots of good bread and cheese and cold meat and salad, maybe a few cans of soup.'

'The bed is a bit overwhelming. If you fell out of that thing you'd break a leg.'

They sat on the edge of the high bed and bounced solemnly. Greeve yawned.

'I could do with a couple of hours' sleep right now, to make up for last night.'

'Carry on. I'll go back into the village and do the shopping.'

Greeve yawned again. 'It would be better if we stuck together.'

Lisa put her arms round his neck and kissed him. 'We're safe here. We've vanished off the face of the earth. Even we don't know where we are. Get some sleep.'

Ryder called Lacey.

'I'm in Valence. Any news?'

'Yes. They've gone to ground. A cottage near a farm, which suggests they may be planning to stay for at least a week. It would appear to be a reasonably isolated spot with plenty of cover. I get the impression that if you were to finalize the deal soon it would be at least several days before the news broke. Do you have a road map with you?'

'Yes.'

'Right: find Sisteron first....'

· **Twelve** ·

'Alan. Wake up.'

Greeve opened his eyes and blinked at Lisa, sitting on the bed with her hand on his shoulder. It took him a moment to remember where he was.

'You've been asleep all afternoon. I thought I'd better waken you in case you couldn't get to sleep tonight.'

'Thank you.'

'The shower works beautifully and dinner is ready. I've surpassed myself. Real *cordon bleu* bread and cheese.'

'You look terrific. Come here.'

She laughed and slipped out of his grasp. 'Later. I decided we should try to give the impression we're on holiday.'

Her feet were bare, her shorts very short and she wasn't wearing anything under the white running vest. There was a lot of tawny skin showing and it all looked good. She had used a rubber band to fix her hair in a pony-tail and could easily have passed for a sixteen year old. A very sexy sixteen year old.

'You're gorgeous. I love you.'

'Do you know what gorgeous means?'

'Beautiful.'

'That's what it's come to mean.' She leaned against the door with her hands in the pockets of her shorts, one bare foot on top of the other. 'Originally it meant having a beautiful neck. Same root as gorge. There you go.'

'You have a beautiful neck all over. Are you sure you wouldn't like to …?'

'Of course I would, but I'm hungry.'

'So am I. Ten minutes.'

He showered and changed into the Levis and golf shirt and trainers from the bottom of his case. When he went through to the living-room he found the table spread with an assortment of mismatched dishes full of shredded lettuce and spring onions, tomatoes and peppers and olives, half a dozen cheeses, fresh crusty bread and yellow butter, sardines, fruit and a bottle of chilled white wine.

'This looks delicious.'

'It should. I've been slaving over a hot stove all day. Well, I made coffee.'

They ate and drank, not hurrying the meal. There was a marvellous atmosphere of lightheartedness and intimacy about everything they did, as if they had somehow overcome a great danger and were safe and could relax and enjoy themselves. It was good to see her smile again.

Afterwards they went out into the late afternoon sun and paddled in the river and splashed each other and went for a walk down the bank, stopping occasionally for a moment of intimacy. Lisa's vitality was infectious, the sunlight soft on her smooth skin, the movement of her breasts under the wet cotton erotic.

'Let's do it here,' Greeve said, pointing to a grassy hollow among some twisted bushes.

'In the open?' She looked astonished.

'People do. Have you never done it in the open?'

'In San Francisco? We use cars. Less chance of being mugged.'

'I didn't have that problem.'

'Tell me about doing it in the open.'

Greeve laughed. 'You don't want to know. It would spoil your perception of nooky al fresco.'

'Tell me.'

'The first time, I was thirteen, she was fifteen. We did it in the plots, on the grass path between a row of spuds and a pile of dung. It cost me two Beanos and most of a Milky Way. Her knickers were so raggy she didn't have to take them off.'

'What language is this? Explain.'

He explained, amending the story in the telling to take account of the fake legend he had created for himself.

'She was one of the village girls, the kind I wasn't supposed to know. Her name was Norma and she had red hair and freckles and I sometimes wonder what she's doing now. Probably still working in horticulture.'

Lisa giggled and looked up and down the wooded valley. 'I wouldn't be comfortable. I'd be worried about someone watching us. Anyway, you're not armed.'

'That's true. Let's go back.'

She hadn't meant firearms, but the reminder had struck home with Greeve. They had managed to elude pursuit but he still felt the need for a weapon. Just as insurance. The cottage was invisible from the road and the valley was silent and peaceful in the sunshine and he felt safe and anonymous, but it would have been good to have the little extra confidence a weapon brings.

When they reached the cottage Lisa looked at the remains of the meal. 'I should clean up.'

'Later. We'll make love then get up and eat what's left. A salad always leaves me hungry.'

He took her hand and led her through to the bedroom. In her bare feet she barely came up to his shoulder. It was like seducing a child. She began to pull off the white vest but he stopped her.

'Keep it on. At least for now. It's sexy.'

*   *   *

Ryder memorized the map carefully, as he had been taught by the Army: main features first, lines of communication and rivers and river crossings and uplands, then the areas between the main features, the areas of habitation, vegetation, contours, distances, building up a three-dimensional picture of the topography. He closed his eyes and imagined himself moving from the hotel up the road, leaving the road half a mile before the bridge, moving downhill through the trees to the river, following the river uphill towards the cottage shown as a tiny black rectangle. He opened his eyes and followed the route on the map, checking that he had missed nothing.

Outside, car doors slammed as people left after dinner. Noisy French voices. It was a small hotel but it seemed to have a reputation for good food. Ryder had eaten sparingly because experience had taught him that an overfull stomach was not a good start to a period of stress.

He checked the automatic pistol and suppressor passed to him in the bar by the unpleasant little oik with the roll-ups. No one had spotted the exchange and they had said nothing to each other. At the briefing in London the previous night Jackson had told him the tail would locate the targets, deliver the weapon and clear the area and that he would then be on his own.

The gun was a Walther P4, 9mm, eight-round magazine. It wasn't new, but it was in perfect condition, carefully serviced and maintained. He had orders to lose it when the job was done, which seemed a pity.

Dark-blue jeans, dark-blue sweatshirt, black trainers, black socks. He had a black silk balaclava and black leather gloves in his pocket. He stowed the silencer in his jeans and the automatic in his belt and checked his watch.

It would take about an hour and a half to reach the cottage if he moved at a steady pace up the wooded valley. He wanted to arrive at about two, when Godunov and Castelle would be asleep. A few minutes in the house and he would be back in the hotel before dawn.

Time to move.

They had made love slowly, self-indulgently, for a long time, then Lisa had fallen asleep and Greeve had lain awake relishing the physical and mental peace, thinking of the future.

Lisa was his future. Nothing could change that. Living together or married, children or no children, in England or America, the details didn't matter; what mattered was being with this woman for the rest of his life.

But before they could do that there was the problem of the people she had antagonized. Was he being paranoid in thinking there should have been some kind of set-up waiting for them at Georges Ferrat's apartment and that something had gone wrong with the timing? Perhaps what he had seen had been some friend of the pilot's, or someone come to collect money owing; the landlord, perhaps. The killing of Bodo Roth was irrelevant, an official matter; the killing of Lisa's father had again been official, unrelated to the matter of her investigations, whatever she thought. But she had probably made enemies and she might be in danger and they would have to do something about that. Tomorrow they would go through her notebooks and try to get a line on whoever was most likely to be afraid of what she might reveal. They hadn't spoken of the problem since the previous morning, not wanting it to intrude on their happiness.

The nagging disquiet about being in love with the daughter of someone he had killed rose to the surface of his thoughts and he pushed it back down again, knowing he was afraid to examine the dangers too closely. She would never learn what he had done, and after all these years and all these contracts he had come to terms with guilt and doubt and death. He could handle it. Especially if he didn't think about it.

He wasn't ready for sleep, and he was hungry. He slid carefully out of bed, dressed and went through to the living-room and made a supper of the bread and cheese and the remains of the salad, washed down with a glass of wine. Satisfied, he switched off the light and went to the door and listened to the sound of the river and looked up at the stars and the silhouettes of the trees against the sky.

It would be good to live here with Lisa.

What would he do if they lived here, or somewhere like this? The money in the bank in Switzerland would last a long time; it would be possible to live off the interest, if the expenses weren't too high. And Lisa would have her writing; not the book about her investigations, but the novel she had shyly admitted to be working on.

But maybe this life would be too quiet for her, too peaceful. She was a city girl, a San Franciscan; living here might be too much of a culture shock for her. Better to keep this place for the holidays, a place to visit to revive old memories.

He thought of her lying asleep in the big bed, warm and soft and smelling of love, naked and smooth and needing his arms around her.

Ryder moved silently downhill through the trees, skin alert to the touch of branches and the changes in temperature as the slight breeze came down the valley, bringing the scent of pine and dewed grass. It took him back to the days of his training rather than to any actual battlefield. The Falklands hadn't been like this. The Falklands had been wet and cold and the smell he remembered was the sourness of long-dead vegetable matter rotting into peat, disturbed by their boots and the occasional exploded shell. He had no good memories of the South Atlantic.

He stopped and looked up at the hill on the far side of the valley, trying to judge his position from the black shape silhouetted against the soft sky. Somewhere below him the river murmured and muttered to itself on its way downhill over the stones and between the rocks. His feet were already wet with dew. He checked that the automatic was still tucked safely into the back of his waistband and moved on. Now and then he disturbed a bird but the slight sound of their wings would be inaudible in the cottage.

He thought about Godunov and Castelle. Were they actually married or were they lonely KGB agents who had sought comfort and reassurance in each other's arms as an antidote to the loneliness and isolation of their chosen profession? Were they lying in bed right now, believing themselves safe in their hidden French farm cottage, seeking a moment of happiness, a brief respite from lives of tension and fear and treachery? No, not treachery. Ryder had never gone with the accepted view that spies were dirty, treacherous people. Reverse the situation: imagine British agents alone in Russia or Iraq, risking everything for their country; they weren't dirty or treacherous. They were incredibly brave, incredibly dedicated. Theirs was the real courage, the courage needed to act alone, deep in enemy territory, unarmed, surrounded by suspicious eyes. If a British spy was brave, so was a Russian spy.

Which didn't make them any less dangerous.

His feet sank into soft ground and he felt the cold of the water seeping into his shoes and swore silently. He seemed to be disturbing large numbers of flying creatures which sought out the exposed areas of flesh. He took the silk balaclava and leather gloves from his pocket and pulled them on.

A light!

He dropped into a crouch and watched the yellow rectangle through narrowed eyes, trying not to lose his night vision. It was several hundred yards away and had to be one of the windows of the cottage. He kept the tiny area of brightness in the periphery of his vision until it went out twenty minutes later, then checked the luminous dial of his watch. Just after midnight. They had probably been having it off then they'd got up for coffee or something to eat or a shower and now they would be back in bed and by the time he reched the cottage they would be asleep. He moved off again, angling down the slope, aiming for a point on the river bank about a hundred yards below the cottage.

This was good. This was what he had been trained for, this was what he had sweated for and worked at and imagined. The Army had been a good training ground, but there had been too many men, too much organization, too much noise, too much equipment, too many orders, too many restrictions. There had been no chance for a man to exercise his initiative, his individuality, his own way of doing things.

Jackson had been pleased by his first two kills, but they had been routine, probably a test. The little man with the balding head and the jewellery and the dry manner had been complimentary but not particularly impressed. A successful kill here – two kills – would satisfy him. It was important to Ryder that he earn Jackson's respect.

The sound of the river was close now on his left and the ground was levelled out as he reached the valley bottom. The soft earth of the slope had changed to short grass with stones and small rocks in it and the trees had thinned out somewhat. He walked slowly, feeling the sweat trickling down the back of his neck under the balaclava.

What would be his next assignment, his next contract? As Jackson's confidence in him grew, perhaps the contracts would become more difficult, more important, more exciting. It was vital that he absorb every atom of information from the early jobs, so that he could build on his experience and become a reliable and skilled assassin. The money was good and Jackson had hinted that it would become better with time. It was an honourable profession, one Ryder could follow with pride. The one major drawback was the fact that he could never speak of his work to anyone. That had been obvious, but hard to accept. It would have been icing on the cake to be able to drop a few hints to old acquaintances and see the respect and admiration and perhaps even the fear on their faces.

Perhaps, once he was assured and secure in his new profession, he would develop the confidence which would allow him to meet women on equal terms. Perhaps, with three or four successful kills under his belt, he might not be so pathetically tongue-tied and terrified when one of them spoke to him. Lots of men were still virgins in their late twenties and went on to have perfectly satisfactory relationships with women. Maybe he'd just never met the right girl. It was easy to talk briskly and authoritatively to a platoon of men, but the girls he'd met so far just had to look at him expectantly and his mouth started moving before his brain could get into gear. He sometimes thought back over the ghastly things he had said to women and squirmed with embarrassment at the memories.

The cottage couldn't be far ahead now. He dropped on one knee and tried to spot it silhouetted against the sky. Was that it? Was that a hint of a roof ridge and a chimney? He moved on.

The ground here was relatively level, probably part of the old course of the river, small stones protruding through the short grass. He moved silently, at a slow walk. No sense rushing things at this late stage in the operation.

He knelt again and this time he saw the whole roof and the small chimney at each end and the unmistakable reflection of starlight off the windscreen of a car. He settled gently into a prone position, the grass cool on his stomach, and absorbed information.

They would be asleep by now, but he would give them another half hour just to make sure. It was a small building, probably just two or three rooms. If the door was open, as it probably was, he would move in silently, the pencil torch illuminating the floor, identify the bedroom, enter it, locate the bed and only at the last moment raise the light to show him the position of their sleeping bodies. Two shots into the man's head, two into the woman's. Then back out again....

'Freeze!'

Ryder felt the muzzle of a gun pressed hard against his spine.

'If you so much as breathe I'll blow your central nervous system apart!'

The shock left Ryder dazed. This had to be the Russian, Godunov. His English was perfect, educated but with a touch of some regional accent. Completely convincing. Why the hell was he thinking of irrelevances when the bastard had a gun in his back? Probably for the same reason that at times of trauma people tend to retreat into the mundane activities they can handle safely. He closed his eyes and let his face drop slowly into the wet grass.

'Spread your arms! Wide!'

A hand travelled down his spreadeagled left arm, checking for weapons, then down his right arm, then over his sides and waist. The automatic was located and removed. He heard the rattle of metal on metal and knew the pistol had been loaded and the safety catch moved. He felt a new sensation in the middle of his back.

'Christ! You weren't armed!'

'I am now. Unless you're loaded with blanks.'

Ryder thought of the eight 9mm slugs, each with the little crosscut he had applied with his Swiss Army knife, and exhaled shakily into the wet grass. Was this to be the last thing he would experience, this cool dampness on his face?

The probing hand found the silencer and went on to check out the rest of him, all the way down to his ankles. This man knew what he was doing.

'Over! Gently!'

Ryder rolled slowly on to his back, wondering if this was his chance to grab the gun and go for the balls or the throat.

'Forget it.' The voice came from the darkness several feet away. 'I'm not there.'

The muzzle of the Walther was suddenly jammed hard into the base of his stomach and he gasped with pain.

'If you twitch I fire. Believe me.'

'I hear you!'

The hand checked him out all the way from the top of his head to his ankles.

'Back on your face. Hands behind your back.'

Ryder rolled over onto his side and suddenly lashed out with one leg, going for a sweeping action which would take the legs out from under the figure in the darkness. But the Russian wasn't there. Ryder closed his eyes and tensed involuntarily and waited for the shot.

· **Thirteen** ·

The shot didn't come.

Instead, without warning, a foot was rammed violently up between his thighs into his crotch. His balls seemed to explode and he jerked convulsively into a foetal position, not believing there could be this much pain in the whole world. He wanted to scream but couldn't get air into his lungs. It felt as if the whole of his groin and stomach had been electrocuted. He pressed his face into the ground and felt the tears being squeezed out of his contorted eyes.

Then there was a heavy knee in the middle of his back and one of the hands cupped over his testicles was wrenched away and twisted up to his shoulder-blades and a rope or something was being tied round his wrist. He was incapable of resisting. The other hand was dragged back and the two wrists lashed together.

'On your feet.'

He tried to speak but it was almost impossible. 'Can't.' A pathetic croak.

He was seized by a powerful hand and lifted bodily to an upright position. He squealed in agony and would have collapsed again but for the remorseless grip forcing his arms up his back. Bitter acid filled his throat and he felt for a moment as if he were about to throw up.

'Walk.'

The hand was still gripping his contorted arms; the muzzle of the automatic was pressing into the small of his back, pushing him forward. He forced his legs into motion, gritting his teeth against the jolts of fire shooting up through his guts, feeling the sweat soaking the balaclava and going cold. In the darkness there seemed no point in keeping his eyes open. It was easier to squeeze them shut in a futile attempt to suppress the agony.

The walk to the cottage was short but it left him exhausted. He stumbled over the doorstep into the blacker darkness and suddenly the light came on and he blinked at a small room full of heavy furniture and a cooker and a sink; on a table were the untidy remains of a meal. He was turned and pushed into a deep armchair and cried out as his swollen testicles hit the cushion.

He looked up through the haze and compared the face with the photograph he had studied in London the previous night and again in his hotel room tonight just before walking so casually downstairs and out the front door like any innocent man going for a stroll before turning in. He had been so full of confidence, so strong, so *stupid*, just that short time ago.

It was Godunov all right. The Russian looked lean and hard and merciless. He didn't look Russian, somehow; instead he looked very ordinary, self-contained, self-reliant, the sort of man Ryder would have been glad to have under his command. Straight brown hair neatly trimmed, clear complexion, grey eyes, firm mouth. What made him different was his attitude: the bastard had an underlying self-confidence, a competence, a ... what was it?

Shit! The Russian had what Ryder had tried for many years to achieve.

He was unafraid. He was unafraid because he knew he

would win.

He had *authority*.

The silencer was screwed on to the muzzle of the Walther and there was something about the way the Russian held the gun that suggested he had been trained to use it and had used it for real on many occasions. There were no laces in Godunov's trainers. Presumably they were what was now holding Ryder's wrists so painfully together behind his back.

'Alan?' The woman's frightened voice came from the other end of the house. 'Alan?'

'It's all right.' It was a surprise that they didn't speak Russian to each other. But the woman had been born in America; Russian was probably her second language.

She appeared in the doorway, naked, her eyes heavy with sleep, her face showing her fear, her black hair tangled. Her body was magnificent, not an ounce of surplus fat, the breasts firm and upstanding, the muscles of the thighs beautifully defined, the ankles slim, the waist narrow.

'It's all right, Lisa. Get dressed.'

She gasped and vanished back into the darkness. Godunov took hold of the top of the silk balaclava and ripped it off and stared into his face.

'Who the hell are you?'

Ryder shook his head. From now on he would say nothing at all. Not a word. He had been trained. Start talking, even just the odd innocuous word, and it would be hard to stop. Just say nothing. If he could persist long enough Godunov might give up.

'I have all the time in the world.' Godunov poured a glass of white wine and took a mouthful. 'We're a long way from the farm, so no one will hear if you scream and anyway you'll have your poncey balaclava stuffed in your mouth when I start hitting your balls. I've tied your hands

very tightly, probably too tightly, so after a while they'll
go black and start rotting. And I'm not going to give you
anything to drink, so your liver and kidneys will very
quickly go toxic. I think that takes only a day or so. After a
few hours you'll tell me everything I want to know and
you'll realize you should have told me immediately,
before all the damage was done. So use the head. I'm not
even particularly interested in who you are: what I want
to know is who you're acting for.'

The woman came back into the room. She had pulled
on shorts and a running vest and somehow looked even
more desirable. Maybe if a woman like this had been
friendlier some time in the past he wouldn't be here now.
With someone like Lisa Castelle at home he wouldn't
have wanted to get involved in this lunatic job.

'Who is he?' Her accent was American.

'He hasn't told me yet. But he will. Could you make
some coffee, please, Lisa. Two cups, just, for you and me.
Don't get within range of his feet.'

Ryder blinked and shook his head to stop the beads of
sweat running into his eyes. The movement was enough
to send a spasm of agony through his stomach. He could
hear the woman filling a kettle behind him and realized he
desperately wanted a drink. His mouth and throat were
already painfully dry.

'What happened? Did you hear him?'

Godunov shook his head. 'I got up for some supper
then wandered outside to enjoy the night. I was just about
to come back in when I heard birds flying. Something had
disturbed them. In our present circumstances I had to be
suspicious. I was expecting him, he wasn't expecting me,
so it was easy. I take it you don't recognize him?'

'No.'

Ryder flinched as the Russian straightened up from
where he was leaning against the table. The muzzle of the

Walther was jammed into his stomach and he groaned as a rough hand searched the pockets of his jeans.

'So you're staying at a hotel.' Godunov examined the key and its orange plastic tab. 'I think this is the hotel a couple of miles down the road from the village. Room 6. I wonder what we'd learn if we had a look through your things.'

The bastard was watching his face closely and must have seen the involuntary reaction. His wallets were there, of course, the passport Jackson had supplied – and his pencilled notes and the two photographs, the material he had sworn to Jackson would be destroyed before he moved in on the target. He had been so keen not to screw up, so desperate not to forget anything, and now being careful was about to ruin everything.

'So: a quick visit to your room might supply a lot of the answers.' Godunov sat down and studied him thoughtfully. The kettle boiled. The Russian waited while the woman made the coffee and passed him a cup. Ryder would have given anything for a mouthful of coffee.

Godunov sipped and put his cup on the table and sat back.

'I don't think we need you any more. If you're not going to talk and the information we need is in your room then you're automatically redundant. An encumbrance. A liability.' Give the bastard his due, his English was faultless. Well, the vocabulary was faultless; the accent was suspect. It was as if he had learned his English from someone with a strong regional twang and was now working on improving it.

Ryder swallowed, trying to moisten his throat. 'A lot of people know I'm here. If I don't call in within the next few hours they'll come looking for me. And you.'

'We won't be here.'

'What will they find? My body? What do you think will happen then?'

Godunov shook his head. 'They won't find your body. There's a lot of country around here. You might not be found for years.'

'They'll catch up with you sometime.'

The Russian shrugged. 'They won't know where to look. I think we're just wasting time here.'

The woman walked across and paused at the door.

'Alan. Please.'

Godunov rose and followed her. He stopped at the door and looked back.

'We'll be outside, watching you through the window. If you try anything, I'll see you.' He raised the Walther menacingly and went out.

Ryder closed his eyes and sank back in the armchair. He was beginning to shiver, and it was not the shivering that comes with cold.

Outside, Greeve glanced through the window at the man in the armchair; he appeared to have accepted his situation with a degree of fatalism.

Lisa's voice was shaking. 'Who is he, Alan?'

'I don't know.'

'Did he really come here to kill us?'

'Nothing else makes sense. For some reason, I'd expected it to be a Frenchman, or maybe an American. Shows you the dangers of making assumptions.'

Lisa clung to his arm and rested her head on his shoulder. 'I can't relate to all this. It's unreal. I can't really accept that people are trying to kill us. I'm terrified. We'll have to go to the police.'

'You'll need hard evidence.'

'Evidence? My God, Alan, what's that sitting in there if it isn't evidence?'

'A man out hunting in the middle of the night. An odd way of doing it, and hardly the most suitable weapon, but people do some strange things and the courts have to listen.'

'Oh, come on!'

'Has he admitted he was looking for us?'

'Not directly, I suppose.'

'Has he admitted trying to kill us?'

'No, but....'

'Did he fire this weapon at us?'

'No, of course not, but....'

'Has he threatened us in any way?'

'No.'

'Is he carrying anything connecting us to him?'

'No, but perhaps in his room....'

'Exactly. We need to see what he has in his room.'

'The police could do that.'

'Think of this: if we go to the police and they believe us and he's arrested – which may not necessarily happen – we'll have to hang around interminably while they carry out an investigation. We might even have to wait for a trial. What happens then? Do you think whoever sent him will stop there? Or will they go on trying to kill us? They'll be even more desperate to silence you, and me too in case I know anything.'

He felt her beginning to sob on his shoulder, felt her despair and her fear, and wished it really were possible for them to go to the police and dump the whole thing in their hands and ask for protection. But his own fake legend would never stand up to the inevitable intense examination; a few routine enquiries would quickly establish that Alan Sinclair did not actually exist and the rule had always been that he could not call on Heward for help. Lisa was above suspicion but he would almost certainly find himself in a cell while further investigations were carried out and then she would be on her own, without his protection, a sitting duck, with the enemy frantic to silence her. He had to steer clear of the police: he and Lisa had to remain free and mobile and elusive.

Inside, the man in the armchair moved, trying to ease himself into a more comfortable position. Greeve tapped the silencer twice on the glass of the window and the man stopped and lay back, eyes shut, his face shiny with sweat.

'So what do we do, Alan?'

'We're struggling from lack of information. We don't know who the enemy is. If we had that information you could go public, write an article, get it published; then they wouldn't dare go anywhere near you.'

'He won't have that kind of information in his room.'

'You never know. I was watching his face when I found the room key: he was shocked. He realized he'd made a bad mistake.'

'Can you get into the hotel just now?'

'Not right now. Too dangerous. It will have to be in the morning. I'll get dressed up and try to look like someone who has every right to be there. It's always the best way.'

Lisa sniffed and wiped her face on her vest. 'Alan, there are times when you don't act or sound like an innocent art dealer. Like tonight. I wonder about you. Maybe you're like Dad.'

'In what way?'

'He worked for the CIA.'

'*What?*'

Lisa sniffed again. 'Oh, he wasn't one of your agents with guns and codes and a radio in the heel of his shoe; he wasn't a full-time employee. But I do know he kept his eyes and ears open when he was abroad in sensitive areas and talked to people when he got back, and I'm fairly sure he carried stuff back and forward for them. He reckoned it wasn't unusual among journalists and people like that. He didn't tell me everything, and what I'm telling you is a secret. But I'm beginning to wonder if you may be … you know.'

Greeve was silent, his mind racing, trying to recognize the implications of this startling revelation. He'd have to think about it. Carefully. But later.

'We'd better get this guy sorted out. The laces I tied round his wrists are probably too tight, and I should fix his legs as well. We'll have to secure him for a few hours at least, until I've been to the hotel.'

'So you're not actually going to kill him.'

'Of course not.'

'You sounded as if you meant it. You had me scared.'

'It was important that he believed it. I had to believe it myself, just for a moment, or he'd have recognized I was bluffing.'

When he killed this man, it would be quietly, out of Lisa's sight. She must never know.

Lisa followed him into the room. The man in the chair opened dull eyes and looked at them, trying to read the message in their faces.

Greeve stood over him, the pistol in his hand. 'I'm going to keep you alive till I see what's in your room, in case I have to ask you any questions.'

'I think my hands are already dead. I can't feel anything.'

'I'll deal with that.'

Greeve used the cable from Lisa's hair drier to lash the man's ankles to the legs of the armchair then, working from behind, retied the laces round his wrists, loosening them slightly but without creating an opportunity for him to wriggle free. The hands were purple and swollen, but the damage did not look to be permanent.

'Go to bed, Lisa. I'll stay here.'

'I won't be able to sleep.'

'You'll be surprised.'

*   *   *

Greeve woke her at nine o'clock with coffee and hot croissants and butter. She sat up and blinked at him.

'I did sleep. I wouldn't have believed it. How about you?'

'He fell asleep, so I grabbed the chance of some shuteye. Listen: while I'm away you'll have to stand guard. You'll have to look as if you know how to handle the gun.'

'I do. I did a training course in self-defence and firearms. It was Ralph's idea. He didn't want me being raped. I have a handgun at home.'

'Can you use this one?'

'Show me how.'

It took only a minute to familiarize her with the weapon.

'I don't think I could kill anyone.'

'If he gets dangerous, point and shoot. Don't hesitate. He'll kill you if he gets the chance. Eat your breakfast then spell me while I shower and get dressed.'

The man in the chair looked grey but otherwise healthy. The skin on his hands had returned to something approaching its proper colour.

'I need to go.'

'What?'

'I need a run-off.'

'Christ!' Greeve stared at him in dismay. 'Come on, then. But if you try anything....'

'I won't.'

The easiest way to do it was to free his legs and lead him to the bathroom, then drop his trousers and allow him to perform in a sitting position.

'If you crap, don't ask me to wipe your ass.'

'I'm very thirsty.'

Greeve gave him two glasses of water from the sink then fastened his trousers and led him back to the armchair and began securing him.

'I'm going to your hotel now. Lisa will keep an eye on you. If you try anything, she will kill you. Understand?'

'Yes.'

'Don't make the mistake of thinking that because she's a woman she's less capable than I am.'

'I know better.'

'What does that mean?'

'You know what I'm talking about.'

'Tell me.'

'Sod off.'

It was a short journey to the small hotel set back from the roadside a mile or two south of the village. The day was sunny and rapidly becoming hot and when Greeve pulled into the car-park and switched off the engine there was an air of Sunday morning lethargy about the place. Several people sat in the shade reading newspapers; two little girls in shorts and bare feet chased each other in and out of the bushes; a family carrying a packed lunch argued without heat then drove off slowly.

Greeve straightened his tie and walked in through the front door carrying his jacket over his arm. The hall was empty. There was the smell of coffee and distant cooking. He walked unhurriedly up the stairs and followed the little sign to the right. Room 6 was at the end of the short corridor. He slipped the key into the lock and entered without a sound and locked the door behind him.

· **Fourteen** ·

Ryder's bed hadn't been slept in but the cover was still turned down, so it was likely that the chambermaid had still to make her rounds. Greeve rumpled the sheets and made an indentation in the pillow to suggest that the occupant had spent the night there then began his search, not stopping to study anything in detail. When he left a few minutes later he was carrying several items in his jacket pockets and was satisfied that he had missed nothing.

He stopped the car at the roadside before he reached the bridge over the river and went through everything carefully in case there was anything Lisa should not see, then drove on and arrived back at the cottage just an hour after leaving. Lisa met him at the door. Greeve read her face.

'Did he give you any trouble?'

'No. I gave him some coffee and bread and butter. What did you find?'

'I'm still trying to work it out. Come on.'

He took the gun and sat at the cleared table and laid out the things he had found in the hotel room. The man in the chair watched stone-faced.

'Wallet: our man's name is David K. Ryder; address in Earls Court. That's London. Drives a Rover. Member of the RAC. Bank cards, credit cards, all very normal. But the passport he's carrying is in the name of Malcolm Stevenson and there's a second wallet with a completely different set of papers and cards to back it up. The car-hire documents indicate this is the name he is using at the moment. Right so far, Mr Ryder?'

Ryder didn't raise his eyes from the empty fireplace. His mouth was set in a grim line.

'About a thousand pounds in cash, French and British, some of it in the wallets, some of it tucked into the toe of a shoe in his case. Seems rather a lot for an honest man to be carrying. A spare magazine for a Walther P4. A Swiss Army knife. And then we come to the interesting stuff.'

Greeve displayed two photographs. 'A very good shot of you, Lisa, not such a good shot of me. Yours is cut from the dust cover of your book, mine appears to have been taken covertly in a bar some years ago. I can't quite place where or when, but it's a long time since I owned this jacket or this shirt. And in this notebook I find a little map showing how to get to this cottage from Valence, which is a town on the main Marseille-Paris road about fifty miles west of here. And on this page, your name, Lisa, with a brief description of you: height, weight, hair colour, age, and the comment *Very beautiful*. I like that. On the next page, a similar description of someone I suspect is me, but I'm not described as being very beautiful. What it says is V.D. I don't think that's a reference to a social disease, is it, Mr Ryder?'

'It means Very Dangerous, Mr Godunov.'

'Very dangerous, Mr Godunov. And the name on the page is Mikhail Godunov. And against both our names, Lisa, are the initials KGB. What do you make of this?'

She stared at him and silently held out her hand for the notebook. He gave her the photographs as well. She studied them for a long time, her brow furrowed, then handed them back.

'What the hell is going on, Alan? I honestly don't understand.'

'I think I do,' Greeve said quietly.

Lisa watched his face intently. 'What do you know?'

'I haven't put it all together yet; there are still some things puzzle me. But what do I know for certain? I know this man came here to kill us. Why else would he be crawling around out there in the middle of the night in dark clothing, wearing a black balaclava and gloves, armed with a silenced automatic pistol? Nothing else makes sense, whatever a court might be persuaded to think by a clever defence counsel. I know he accepted a contract to do so: he was provided with photographs of us, and details of our descriptions and where to find us, which means he had no idea who we were until someone contracted him to kill us. It's almost certain he'd never even heard of us until a few days ago and has no personal animosity towards us. I should imagine he was zeroed in on us, supplied with the gun and left to get on with it.'

Lisa looked at Ryder. 'Is this true?'

'Work it out for yourself.' Ryder was apparently fascinated by the empty fireplace.

'Does that mean yes?'

Ryder shrugged impatiently.

Lisa looked back to Greeve. 'So what's all this about the KGB and ... Godunov, was it?'

'That was his motivation. Presumably Mr Ryder is an honourable man and needs adequate motivation before he can carry out a contract. He kills for money, but he has to believe that the people he kills are valid enemies, people worth killing. Someone has persuaded him that we are Russian spies. I am Mikhail Godunov, you are ... I'm not sure who you are. The only name here is Lisa Castelle.'

'Not all Russian spies have Russian names.' There was a hint of self-reassurance in Ryder's voice, as if he were trying to mask his own doubts.

They stared at him. He seemed to have recovered a good deal of his composure. He looked like a man who had decided to accept his fate and would do his best to behave with dignity. Lisa glanced at Greeve and back to the man in the chair.

'But who's paying you? Who issued the contract? Who wants us dead?'

'No comment.'

'Do you know?'

'No comment.'

'Was it Carver Arms?'

Ryder's blank look told its own story.

'I used to know a man,' Greeve said slowly. 'I'd known him at school, which was why he told me things he wouldn't have told anyone else. He was an assassin. A professional killer. He worked for the government.'

'Which government?' Lisa's eyes were wide with astonishment.

'The British Government. He probably worked for MI6, but no one had ever confirmed that, so even he wasn't sure. His money was paid in cash, he had no formal connection with anyone, no pension scheme, never met anyone except the one man who controlled him.'

'You had a friend who was a murderer?' Lisa seemed to be sinking defensively into her chair.

'The friends you make at school stay friends all your life.' Greeve unscrewed the silencer then screwed it back on again. 'As I said, he was an honourable man. Not so much a murderer as an assassin. Highly skilled. Conscientious. A man who took pride in his work. A Civil Servant, if you want. He did an unpleasant job, but lots of people have jobs like that, and do them well.'

'You had a friend in MI6?' Ryder's tone was derisive. 'The KGB, you mean.'

Greeve shook his head. 'No, I mean what I say. I even met my friend's boss, once, by accident. Little chap, very posh, fair hair going bald, lots of jewellery. A snob. Much given to the wearing of double-breasted suits and club ties. Gold propelling pencil, gold cigarette case. Said his name was Heward, but that may not have been true.'

He was watching Ryder's face carefully and saw the shock of recognition, immediately suppressed.

'I'm getting hungry,' Greeve said. 'I've had nothing but a salad since yesterday. What's in the larder?'

'Hardly anything.' Lisa seemed thankful for this abrupt return to the mundane. She went to the fridge and looked inside. 'We'll have to stock up. If we're staying.'

'We'll be here for a while at least. I should have thought to buy some food while I was in the village.'

'I could go and get something.' Her eagerness to get out of the cottage was transparent.

'Please. Some wine as well, and get me a pack of cigarettes.'

'You don't smoke.'

'I do occasionally. I'd like one now.'

It took her only a few minutes to change and brush her hair and come back asking for the car keys.

'I'll be back as quick as I can.'

'No rush.'

The two men listened to the sound of the car being driven away then Greeve stood up, the pistol hanging loosely from his hand.

'It's that time, Mr Ryder.'

'What time?' Ryder was doing a good job of controlling his fear.

'You know what I mean.'

*   *   *

It was a relief to get away from the cottage, away from the man who had come to kill her and Alan, away from the ugly automatic pistol and its obscene silencer, away from that awful atmosphere of menace, away from the smell of Ryder. It was a relief to be in the illusory safety of the car, driving along a narrow French road on a brilliant French Sunday morning, down a wooded valley to a sleepy little French village to buy food and wine.

She'd known Alan only a week, so it wasn't surprising that she still had a lot to learn about him, and maybe some of the things she learned would be surprising. Like his astonishing ability to overcome a professional killer, for instance; like his unexpected familiarity with automatic pistols; like his having a British Government assassin for a friend; like his calm readiness to burgle a hotel room; like the air of authority he had assumed so easily when things got rough.

Maybe all this was part of what made him so fascinating. Hidden depths. Reserves of power. Total self-confidence but without the irritating air of superiority that usually comes with it in men. He had never once said anything about himself which might be thought of as boasting; if anything, he seemed determined to make himself look like a bit of a fool, at least if the story were likely to make her laugh. If she'd had to describe him to a friend she would have said he was intelligent and good-humoured and diffident, with a dry wit and the knack of making a woman feel good by giving her his undivided attention.

Was she blinded by love? If she was, she liked being blind. There had never been anyone like Alan in her life, never anyone who set her on fire the way he did, never anyone who made her feel so important and valuable and relaxed and passionate and complete. And clever. With Ralph she had quickly learned to keep her opinions to herself because they always amused him or irritated him. Educating the uneducated was his job, he had been fond of declaring, but he had an unfortunate habit of bringing his work home with him. Alan prompted her instead of correcting her. He was a good listener, and when he made a point it was clear that he was thinking about what she was saying and looking at her premise from unexpected angles, as if wanting to build on her ideas instead of demolishing them. Sometime soon, when their life was more peaceful, she would ask him to read her novel and help her with it. He was incredibly well-read.

When their life was more peaceful....

Alan would sort it out. He would take care of her. He would help her find out who was trying to kill her and then she would plaster it all over one of the big dailies and it would be taken up by the television stations and then the other papers and then they would be safe. They would have official protection and anyway the other side wouldn't dare come near them. The armour of publicity.

But please let it happen soon.

She drove into the village and parked. The small shop was open, cool and dim and heavy with the scents of coffee and fruit and strong tobacco and bread and rubber boots.

The little café-restaurant was open as well and the buttered croissants earlier had merely whetted her appetite. She took her time over coffee and a huge sandwich, savouring the momentary release from the tension of the past few hours.

As she drove back she found herself checking the rear-view mirror, looking for a tail. There was only one vehicle behind her, a camping van with mountain bikes strapped to the roof and what looked like most of a grade class inside. She let the van overtake just before the bridge and watched it vanish up the hill before she turned onto the track leading down past the farm to the cottage.

When she stopped and got out Alan appeared at the door. He had changed back into his jeans and a blue and white checked shirt and trainers.

'Hullo.' His smile was relaxed.

'Hi. Everything OK?'

'Yes, no problem. I'll give you a hand with that lot.'

She followed him into the cottage and stopped. The armchair was empty and he had been fitting the cable back on to her hair dryer.

'I'm afraid the cable's going to be a bit short. I had to cut it in half, remember, and I've no insulating tape to make a join safe. I'll buy you a new one first chance I get.'

'Where is he?'

'I let him go.'

'What!'

He shrugged. 'We talked. I proved to him that we're not Russian and that seemed to take the wind out of his sails. He gave me a little information, enough to work on. I'm pretty certain he didn't actually know the real reason for the contract. He realized he had been manipulated and I think that offended him; as I guessed earlier, he's an honourable man and he's very angry that he was lied to by his masters. We reached an agreement. I cut him loose and gave him his money back and told him that if I ever saw him again I would assume he was making another attempt on our lives and God save him if he did.'

The Walther was lying on the table. Lisa felt a strong urge to pick it up and sniff the end of the barrel to see if it had been used.

'Are you telling me the truth, Alan?'

'Yes, I am.'

'I want to believe you, but....'

'But you think I've killed him and hidden his body somewhere in the woods?'

She made a gesture. 'I'm sorry, but....'

He nodded, his face serious. 'I can understand. I suppose I'd react the same way under the same circumstances. Put your suspicions on hold for the moment; maybe I'll be able to find some way of proving I'm telling the truth.'

'We could go down to the hotel and speak to him. Even just see him.'

He glanced at his watch. 'That would do the trick, but I want to get out of here as quickly as possible. In fact, I think we should move right now. I'd rather not be here if it turns out I've misjudged him. It's time we vanished again, and properly this time. We may have survived one attack, but it doesn't mean the war's over.'

His urgency was infectious, reawakening her fears. She wanted to protest, but she wanted to trust him. It was so important that she could trust him.

He looked at her sideways then put an arm round her shoulder. 'Cheer up.'

'I'm a bit uptight. It's not every day I find a man with a gun trying to kill me.'

She slipped out of his arm on the pretext of emptying the paper bags. Maybe she should pretend her period was due; then she wouldn't have to make love to him for a while. She couldn't face that, not when there was the distinct possibility she had been in love with a killer.

She noted her own use of the past tense and felt a sudden chill of despair.

They left the food in the fridge, packed their bags and loaded the car. Greeve asked Lisa to take the wheel and instructed her to turn left at the junction with the main road and head west towards Valence.

'Where are we going, Alan?'

'I'm still thinking about that. I'm still trying to work it all out. I'm still trying to work out our priorities.'

'Which are?'

'Still to find out who's trying to kill you.'

'And you.'

'And me.'

'And how are you going to do that?'

'I have an idea. It means you'll have to be dead.' He smiled across the car at her startled expression. 'If they think you're dead they'll stop looking for you. If they think I'm still alive they'll have to come looking for me. Without you to worry about I'll have more freedom of movement.'

'How are you going to convince them I'm dead?'

'That will take a little working out, and I was awake all night and I'm tired. I need some sleep. When you reach Valence, head north for Paris.'

He turned the knob to recline the seat and lay back with his eyes closed. He had a lot of thinking to do, a lot of planning.

It was time to stop running. It was time to start taking the initiative.

· **Fifteen** ·

Lacey found it impossible to concentrate. He lowered his *Sunday Times* and stared at the silent wall phone and then at the kitchen clock. Almost midday. Greasley had called in yesterday evening, the Saturday, confirming that Ryder was close to the target and that the gun had been delivered, and had been told to pull out and return to Marseille. Lacey had been waiting since then, hoping for a call from Ryder, but surely it would have come by now if Greeve and Lisa Castelle had been excised overnight. It was all up to the assassin now, and there was nothing Lacey could do except wait and worry.

He hated this time. If Greeve had been the hatchet man instead of Ryder he would not have been so anxious. Greeve had proved himself again and again over the years. Greeve had been reliable. There had often been delays, long periods with no news, but the calm voice had always come on the phone eventually to report a successful hit and Lacey had learned to trust the former sergeant, although there had never been any possibility of liking him.

He thought back to his own early days in the Service, the days when he had been at the sharp end, the man with the sniper rifle or the silenced pistol, the man with the mud on his clothes and the sweat cold on his back.

Had his masters sat in silent offices back in London and cursed him for not calling in? Had they regarded him as an expendable weapon? Had they been more concerned for their own welfare than his?

Definitely.

He stared blindly at the page of newsprint and remembered East Berlin on a bitter winter night in 1976. The target was a young man – Haack? Hauff? The name didn't matter now, just as the reason for the kill didn't matter. What had mattered to Lacey was the slow realization, as he shivered in the black, unheated room overlooking the yard behind the garage, that this was the kind of job that could be handled by any reasonably intelligent minion with weapons training. A fairly good public school and Cambridge qualified him for something better than this. And with that thought came another: that he had only his masters' word for it that the people he had killed in the past and the one he was going to kill tonight were truly enemies of the State. For all he knew the young man could have been a loyal employee who had rogered the girlfriend of the Head of Berlin Station. The girlfriend had a certain reputation, and Head of Station was notoriously vindictive.

And from those thoughts in the darkness of an East Berlin tenement had grown Lacey's determination to improve his position in the Service and from that determination had evolved his plan for the future.

First there had to be a move from killing to directing killers. That had taken a year to achieve. That was the period when he had studied his superiors so carefully and had gone to so much trouble to make himself like them; the suits, the shirts, the manners, the vocabulary, the discreet evidence of class like the gold watch and the gold cigarette case and the membership of the proper clubs. And, of course, there had been his skilful and unobtrusive assumption of responsibility for the dirty work of assassination. His masters wanted the work done but none of them wanted the responsibility. Lacey had proved himself efficient and reliable and ready to relieve them of that problem and in due course they had promoted him and given him the task of building up his own little operation. It is the same throughout all branches of government: prove you can do a job, especially an unpleasant job, and your boss will happily dump it on you for keeps, even if it means promoting you. After all, he's not paying you out of his own pocket.

The Office believed he ran a string of assassins, and no one had ever asked for proof of where the money had been going for the past fifteen years. They respected his tight security, understood the absolute necessity for a total cut-out between the Office and the assassins. They provided the cash, he paid some of it to his men and kept the rest. In fact, there had only ever been Taggart, for the first year, then Greeve and now Ryder, and Greeve's second kill had been Taggart. Taggart had been flawed, a former mercenary who liked killing for its own sake, a man with a loose mouth, and it had been a relief when Greeve took him out. Greeve had been Lacey's man for the past twelve years, a first-class hatchet man, almost infallible, silent and invisible.

But Greeve was getting on in years and recently it had become more and more difficult to motivate him. Perhaps there was an optimum operational life for an assassin; maybe, as with footballers, the mid-thirties brought a drop in strength and stamina and motivation. So Lacey had recruited Ryder and given him two contracts and the lieutenant had performed adequately and in due course Lacey would have called him to a meeting in a hotel somewhere and briefed him and sent him out to excise Greeve. Greeve never knew who Taggart was, and Ryder would never know who Greeve was.

It had to be done that way. Greeve knew too much to be allowed to go on living. He might become conscience-stricken; he might start drinking; he might have an accident and become delirious and babble out everything he knew; he might get religion and want to expunge his guilt. He had to die.

It was pure chance, still unexplained, that Greeve had become involved with the Castelle woman. It only meant he would die sooner than Lacey had anticipated.

The second part of the plan Lacey had sketched out during that bitter night in East Berlin, the really profitable side of the business, had taken longer to arrange. He had been running his section for five years before he finally had enough information to allow him to make a choice among the half-dozen people he had been studying so carefully for so long.

He had approached Eugene Carver in one of the bars at the London Hilton. The giant American had been engrossed in his newspaper when Lacey sat down beside him.

'Mr Carver. Good morning. I understand you're having a lot of trouble with a gentleman by the name of Picard.'

'Who the hell are you?' Carver had looked round for his bodyguard, but Lacey knew Rossi had gone to collect the car.

'We'll go into that later, Mr Carver. I'm working on the assumption that you'd like to see Robert Picard dead.'

'Hey, asshole, what is this?'

'Just keep your eyes open for news of a nasty accident happening to M. Picard.'

He had given the Texan a cool smile and left and two nights later Greeve, briefed that Picard was working for the Bulgarians, had excised the Frenchman in a warehouse in Paris.

Lacey had gone to Carver's room in the hotel a week later.

'You'll have heard about the sad death of M. Picard.'

'Never heard of the guy.'

'There's no charge. Consider it a free sample.'

Carver had stared at him for a long time in silence then asked for proof. Lacey showed him the photographs he had told Greeve to take of the body. The negotiations had been protracted and Carver had remained suspicious until after the second kill. After that they would both have gone down together if anything had gone wrong and the Texan had grown to trust and rely on Lacey. The big money had come from the intelligence Lacey was able to supply, the names and contacts he could provide, the dangers to Carver's armaments business he could foresee, the areas where potential buyers were having cashflow problems but had sensitive goods to offer instead of money. It had turned into a mutually profitable association.

Thirty thousand feet over the Atlantic, Eugene Carver relaxed at the controls of the Learjet. Rossi was stretched out on one of the seats in the rear with his coat off and his tie loosened, apparently asleep but ready to move in an instant if anything happened; across the aisle the two representatives of the buyers were muttering to each other, heads close together, their swarthy faces intent.

Carver checked the on-board computer. He would be landing at the private field north of Dallas in a little over two hours. There were three pilot's cases full of heroin on the floor between the rear seats: these would be transferred to the cellar of his sprawling ranchhouse, the second half of the electronic missile guidance system would be loaded and he would fly back across the Atlantic to Lisbon, drop the load and the two Iraqis, pick up the second half of the payment in cash, then fly on to London, to meet Lacey and engage in a little rest and recreation.

He liked London. Apart from the business side of things there was a much wider range of women there, all shapes and sizes and nationalities and specialities, and over the years he had developed some very useful contacts, people who understood his need for the intriguing and the exotic. American women were pretty good too, of course, but they all smelled of peppermint. Shut your eyes and it could be the same woman every time, except maybe when he went for one with exceptionally big boobs, like Marcia. Maybe he'd have time to give Marcia a call tonight. A nice oily wallow eased the tensions of a long flight. If only the bloody woman would park her chewing gum before they started....

Carver grinned suddenly, thinking of Lacey. The little fart was still so inhibited, so uncertain, so *English* about screwing around. They had been two years into their business association before Lacey, under the influence of several large whiskies, had finally accepted Carver's invitation to join him in a visit to the house in Bloomsbury. It had been like taking a kid to a toy fair. His first choice had been a silent and rather mousy Danish girl with an inadequate command of the language; presumably she gave him confidence. After that, on subsequent visits, he became much more adventurous. He had a particular fondness for anything coloured. But he still gave the impression of being embarrassed by the subject of sex.

Lisa Castelle should be dead by now, and the man Sinclair. Now, there was a looker; there was one classy lady. It would have been a fine thing to have screwed Lisa Castelle. Small and tight and silky, with a face like off the front cover of a magazine. Intelligent, too, which always added something. She would be only the second

American citizen to be wiped to ensure the security of his operation – her father had been the first – but that was two too many. The wogs and frogs and dagoes were of no account, but he was a patriotic man and didn't like having fellow Americans killed. Especially a beautiful woman. It was her own fault, just as it had been her father's fault. They'd had no call to go interfering in American free enterprise.

It would have been good to have a woman on the plane with him, to make the long hours pass quicker, but he never mixed business with pleasure. Making money required total commitment, one hundred percent attention to detail.

He passed the time calculating, mentally but very accurately the profit he would make from trading the stolen guidance systems for the heroin. He could have made more by setting up a network to sell the H on the streets, of course, but that was someone else's turf and it was dangerous turf. The arrangement he had with the people in the stretch Mercedes was rewarding enough.

Greeve opened his eyes and blinked at the rear of a touring bus. Lisa looked relaxed, her eyes hidden by sunglasses, one arm resting on the sill of the open window.

'Where are we?'

'Somewhere south of Beaune, unless we're on the wrong road.'

He studied the crumpled Michelin map. 'You've done well. You should have wakened me.'

'I enjoy driving. But I was thinking of stopping. I'm thirsty and I need to freshen up. And we need gas.'

'First place you see, then I'll take over.'

'Have you decided yet where we're going?'

'Paris.'

'And then?'

'Then you catch a flight for the States.'

Lisa glanced over at him. 'Why?'

'We have very little to go on, but this Carver Arms and Systems crowd seems like the best bet. You're a journalist, you know how to dig for information without letting on you're doing it. Who are they? Are they legitimate, or are they legitimate but running another operation on the side? Are they engaged in illegal arms dealing? Is there a Mr Carver who's in charge, or is it one of those companies run by a board of directors? Do they have some kind of troubleshooter? Is there anyone who spends time in France or England?'

'Why England?'

'Ryder was English. He was in London just a few days ago, immediately before he came looking for us. He must have talked to someone there. And find out if they have their own air transport. If your pal Georges Ferrat is no longer flying for them they may have their own plane. Anything like that. You know better than I do how to build up a picture of an organization.'

'And what will you be doing while I'm in the States? I take it you're not coming with me?'

She seemed to be accepting the idea. She might actually learn something useful, but what mattered most was that she would be out of the firing line, leaving him free to do whatever was necessary without the problem of having to worry about her safety. Or her disapproval.

'I'll be rooting around in London. I have some ideas, but they're pretty way out. It will take time to find a solid trail.'

Lisa pointed to a sign. 'Service station coming up. This do?'

'Sounds good to me.'

'Will I be safe, do you think?' She said it lightly, but he recognized her fear.

'I'll make a phone call when we stop. I'll spread the word you're dead. That should take the heat off you, with a bit of luck.'

'Who will you talk to?'

'Lady I know who works for one of the tabloids. An old friend. She'll believe me.'

'A close friend?'

He recognized the hint of jealousy in the question and liked the sound of it.

'We had our moments, a long time ago. She's married now with two adopted children.'

'What will you tell her?'

'Enough to get a few paragraphs into the paper about a beautiful but mysterious young woman found dead in a farm cottage in France, and the fact that the American writer Lisa Castelle has been missing for the past week. French police are understood to be putting a blanket of secrecy over the matter while they investigate.'

'The story will be denied sooner or later.'

'The people who matter will be expecting to read the story. They'll believe it. All we need is some time.'

Lisa indicated right and turned into a large service station. She parked at the pumps and Greeve filled the tank then they left the car in the car-park and went into the restaurant. When they had freshened up and eaten he left her over a second cup of coffee and went to the row of phones in the lobby.

'Mr Lomax, please.'

'I'm afraid you have a wrong number.'

'This is Gary Glitter. Mr Lomax, please.'

'I'm afraid you have a wrong number.'

'I'll wait until Hallowe'en.'

'Mr Lomax is not in the office.'

'Thank you.'

He rang Heward's home number. The connection was

made almost instantly. Heward must have been sitting beside the phone.

'Yes?'

'Sorry to call you at home, but it's important.'

A perceptible pause. 'It's all right. Is it an emergency?'

'Perhaps. The young lady we were considering doing business with? I'm afraid she's had an accident.'

'How bad an accident?'

'Couldn't be worse.'

'I see. How did you learn of this?'

'I was there. A gentleman by the name of Ryder is in the same condition.'

Again the pause. 'You're certain of this? How close were you to the accident?'

'I was involved.'

'I didn't realize you had already made contact with the young lady.'

'I met her about a week ago. We had become very close. On a personal basis.'

'I see. This doesn't sound like good business practice.'

'One of those things. You brought her to my attention, remember? She's very attractive and I was attracted. I can only apologize.'

'I remember. This must have been a bad time for you.'

'Very bad. What I want to know is, why was she ... why was she involved in an accident? In view of what we'd discussed.'

'I don't know the answer to that. Perhaps it was something to do with the people she normally did business with. I'll see if I can learn anything.'

'Please do.'

'Where are you now?'

'In transit. Home soon.'

'We should meet. Call me again tomorrow.'

'I'll do that.'

Greeve replaced the phone and went back into the restaurant.

'I think it will work.'

'You spoke to your lady friend?'

'Yes. I pretty well dictated the story for her. She's busy with something else so she won't be able to spend too much time checking. And I said I didn't know precisely where you were supposed to have been found, which will make it all the more difficult for her.'

'So come tomorrow I'll be off the hook?'

'Yes.'

'Thanks. What now? Paris?'

'City of romance and greedy waiters.'

Angela entered the kitchen and took ice from the fridge and dropped it into her gin.

'What's wrong?'

'What?'

'You look like someone stole your skateboard. Who was on the phone?'

'Business. A bit of bad news. Something I'll have to take care of.'

'You looked quite shocked.' She managed to inject a touch of almost genuine sympathy into her voice.

'It's news I hadn't expected. The best laid plans and all that. You begin to wonder if you can trust anyone to do a job properly. If you want something done right, do it yourself.'

'Another night away from home?'

'Probably Tuesday.'

'I'll check the batteries in the vibrator.' She stalked out, letting the door bang shut. Lacey raised a stiff middle finger.

Jesus! Bloody sex! You think you know a man for twelve years and suddenly the bastard does something totally unexpected like taking off after a woman he's only ever seen in a photograph.

It had been a mistake to send Ryder to excise Greeve. His mistake. He had sent a boy on a man's errand. Greeve might be close to the natural end of his peculiar professional usefulness, but his skills clearly hadn't atrophied.

At least the woman was dead. He could reassure Carver of that.

Greeve was now his own problem.

Lacey rose and went upstairs to the small room he used as a study and a retreat from Angela's bitching tongue. He poured a stiff whisky and added a little soda then unlocked the bottom drawer of his desk and lifted out the wooden cigar box. Inside, wrapped in a stained yellow duster, lay a Heckler and Koch P7 K3 and three full 14-round magazines. It had been a long time since he had last used the weapon and he would have to clean it carefully and freshen the oil.

He picked up the phone and tapped out a number.

'The range, please.... Hello, Lacey here. It's time I put in some practice....'

· Sixteen ·

London was wet and chilly, a refreshing change from the heat of France. As already arranged with Lisa, Greeve booked in at a busy commercial hotel at Haringey using the name Geoffrey Canning and stayed in his room, asleep most of the time, until the Monday morning. He visited his bank in the City and asked for his safe-deposit box and exchanged the Alan Sinclair identity for the one in the name of Geoffrey Canning; he also collected the FN High-power automatic pistol and the two 9mm 14-round magazines. The gun he had taken from Ryder was now lying at the bottom of the River Yonne near Auxerre. He rented a Rover and replenished his wardrobe then drove back to the hotel and went up to his room and lay on the bed staring at the ceiling, his face grim, his fingers drumming restlessly on the headboard. After only a few minutes he rose impatiently and paced up and down the carpet for a while then switched on the television and clicked through the channels before switching off again. He glanced through the hotel literature and discovered there was a health club in the basement and went downstairs immediately, relieved to find something to occupy him during this frustrating time of waiting.

He spent the rest of the morning working out in the gym, driving himself until the sweat ran freely, then relaxed in the sauna for an hour before cooling off by ploughing up and down the pool for half an hour. He lunched then went back to his room and slept peacefully for two hours before calling Heward.

'Have you arranged a meet?'

'Yes, but not till Wednesday.' Heward named a hotel in Colchester. 'Your name is Harry Downes, of 18 Bombay Court, Darlington.'

'OK. See you in the bar, usual time.'

'Don't worry if I'm late, Sergeant; I'm very busy just now. I'll be there as soon as I can.'

Lisa smiled and waved to Al Heinz through the glass of his wildly untidy cubicle and he rose and beckoned to her to enter.

'Lisa! You look great. Where've you been? Siddown. Coffee?'

'Thank you. France. Thank you. Please.' It was a game they played. Al had been her first editor and was now a friend and had always had the hots for her, or at least claimed to have. He was a painfully thin man in his mid-forties, the last of his black hair straggling to shoulder-length, his moustache thick and untrimmed.

Lisa picked up a framed photograph from his desk and made a show of counting the number of children.

'Seven? Or have I missed one somewhere?'

'It's only seven.'

'Josey looks great.'

'Maybe if she didn't look so great we wouldn't keep polluting the planet with kids. Cream, no sugar?'

'You remembered.'

'So why the visit, Lisa? I love it, but you're not here because you're missing me.'

'You'd better believe it, Al. I just need a little time on the computers and the library. I'm working on a story. You can have first option if you want.'

'What's it about?'

'Illegal arms dealing. Murder. Like that.'

He sat on the edge of his desk and studied her face shrewdly. 'Taking up where Hugo left off?'

'More or less.'

'You're in dangerous waters, Lisa.'

She nodded. 'I think it got him killed. I'm going to prove it.'

'Let me read what you've written so far.'

'I haven't written anything yet. I have about thirty-five thousand words Dad wrote and a pile of notebooks. I'm still researching. That's why I'm using my feminine charms and the promise of first option to get on to your computers.'

'Help yourself. There's always one free.'

'Thanks, Al.'

'It'll cost you lunch.'

'Can you afford it?'

'Jeez, but you're like your old man! I miss him. He was one of the originals.'

'I miss him too.'

'Mr Houston, sir, calling from Langley.'

'Put him on.' Lacey pursed his pale lips. He had been anticipating the call but not looking forward to it. It had taken him a sleepless night to decide that the safest course would be to give Carver the truth; trying to hide Ryder's failure and the fact that Greeve was still alive might lead to unpleasant complications.

'Hello, my friend.'

'Good afternoon.'

'I'm in Lisbon; on to London tomorrow. Anything to report?'

'The young lady we discussed has retired. Permanently.'

'Good. Very good. And her friend?'

'That's something we should discuss. When do you arrive in London?'

'In time for lunch.'

'I'll see you then.'

'I hope you're not going to give me bad news, my friend.'

How the hell did Carver manage to put so much menace into the word friend?

Lisa called late in the evening. Greeve was watching football on television.

'Hi, Alan. How are you?'

'Fine. Making progress. It's great to hear your voice. I'm missing you. What are you doing?'

'I'm in New York. I pulled the old pals act on an editor friend and I've spent the day using his computers and his library to do a search on Carver Arms. I've learned a lot.'

'Tell me anything that's relevant.'

'I have six sheets of information here, which I'll fax you if you give me a number.'

Greeve found a number on the hotel stationery and read it out to her.

'Give me the gist of it now.'

'OK. It's not a big organization, and it's very much a one-man show. Just twenty-six employees, all based at a warehouse north of Dallas. The boss is Eugene Carver. They don't manufacture arms: they're agents, buying and selling any kind of armaments, vehicles, laser sights, riot-control gear, spares, that sort of thing, with a sideline in renovating and repairing army surplus weapons then selling them. It all looks very honest and above-board and profitable, but hardly profitable enough for Eugene Carver to fly his own Learjet.'

'That takes a lot of money.'

'It surely does. He must be carrying on another business on his own.'

'Don't make the mistake of thinking everything you find confirms your theory. Facts first, then a conclusion.'

'I know, Alan, I know.'

'Go on.'

'I called his firm and asked for him. If he'd been there I'd have said I was selling advertising space in a European magazine, in the hope of finding out if he did much trade there, but he wasn't around. I spoke to a woman, secretary or something. I said I was with Lear and that I was doing a routine customer check, whatever that is, and could I speak to the pilot. She said Carver flies the plane himself and that he left for Europe early this morning, but she didn't know his destination. She gave me the name of the airfield he always uses when he's in England. It's on the fax.'

'That's brilliant, Lisa. That's something I can work on.'

'What will you do?'

Greeve hesitated. He didn't want her flying to England at this time; he didn't want her seeing some of the things he might have to do.

'Is there any way you can check up on dates when he was in England? Or France? Is there any way you could pick up some rumours about his illegal operations? Maybe talk to some legitimate arms people?'

'I could try.' She sounded doubtful.

'Whatever you do, Lisa, don't put yourself in danger. If there's any risk, pull out and vanish.'

'What about you? What are you doing?'

'You remember I spoke to you about an old school friend, the one with the rather unusual occupation?'

'I know who you mean.'

'I called him and I'm meeting him soon. I'm hoping he'll be able to come up with a few ideas. He gets to hear of some very odd goings-on.'

'You'll let me know what he says?'

'Of course.'

'OK.'

'You sound a bit depressed.'

'Jet lag. I didn't sleep much on the plane, and it's been a long day and this hotel is stinking hot and my period's due.'

'Send the fax, get a brandy inside you and go to sleep. We'll talk again tomorrow. Same time.'

'That's a deal. Bye.'

'Bye. Love you.'

She didn't respond. He heard the line go dead and replaced the receiver.

Maybe that was as much as he could expect for the time being. The spectre of Ryder was clearly still hanging over her. It would take time for her to grow accustomed to the possibility that there was now a body buried in soft soil somewhere in a valley in France, killed by the man she had loved and been loved by, the man with whom she had been sharing a bed.

He rose and went downstairs to wait for the fax to come in. When it arrived he went back to his room and sat for a long time trying to extract every last bit of useful information from Lisa's research. Afterwards he lay down on the bed, knowing it would be useless trying to sleep right now with his mind racing, desperately trying to make sense of what he had learned over the past two days.

It would have been good to have Lisa with him now. It would have been good to lie with her nestled in his arms, close and intimate and loving.

He reached out to the bedside cabinet and took the two photographs from his wallet, the photographs Ryder had been carrying. She looked out at him, her hair tightly curled, her big eyes serious, one slim hand under her chin. That was the hand that had stroked him and teased him and sent him cartwheeling with desire. That was the hand....

Enough.

He looked at the photograph of himself. Which hotel bar, and when? He looked quite elegant; obviously an expensive jacket. Possibly.... It was his first Bladen jacket, surely, the one he'd worn for just a short time, until that night in the underground car-park when the big black minder had sprayed the shells around and blown a hole in the shoulder pad....

Which meant....

Get it together, now. Take it slowly. Don't force it. Barcelona. 1987. No, 1986. I flew to Madrid and drove the rest of the way. Rush job. Quick briefing in the hotel in Maidstone. Heward didn't have time to get us rooms. I wore the jacket then.

He stared at the photograph, then closed his eyes tightly and tried to picture the hotel bar.

Maidstone. Old hotel, once a coaching inn. Nice bar. Red brick and old wood.

It was coming back.

Heward in a corner, with a framed watercolour of a landscape on the wall behind him. I was distracted by the watercolour, not listening to Heward, wondering if the stone circle might be the Ring of Brodgar in Orkney.

It had been Maidstone. Definitely. Therefore Heward must have taken the photograph, covertly, maybe using a miniature camera of some kind.

Therefore Heward had passed the photograph to Ryder.

Therefore Heward had contracted Ryder to kill him.

It was confirmation of what he'd already worked out from what he'd learned from Ryder in the cottage but hadn't wanted to believe. Ryder had reacted to his description of Heward but he had refused to accept what had been staring him in the face.

What he had to do now was to link Heward to Carver. Without that link there was no proof that he and Lisa were on the right track. There was a lot he still didn't understand, but it was safe to start from the assumption that Heward had contracted Ryder to excise him. The photographs and notes in Ryder's room, Ryder's reaction to Greeve's description of Heward, the very smell of the familiar gun oil on the weapon Ryder had been carrying, all this pointed directly to Heward. He was uncertain about the reason for the hit but most likely it was because he had outlived his usefulness and knew too many dangerous secrets about Heward. Maybe death was the only possible end for a professional assassin.

Maybe … maybe he himself had excised his predecessor....

The thought brought him upright in his chair. Who had been the first? No, not the Bulgarian. The man hadn't even been able to speak English. Next had been … it was hard to remember. So many contracts, so long ago....

Taggart, the noisy Scot with the scarred face and the skinhead haircut. He'd had the air of a former soldier or mercenary about him. The reason for the contract had seemed perfectly sound at the time, even if he couldn't remember the details: something about Taggart being a link in a chain supplying the IRA with stolen funds.

After Taggart had been.... No, they couldn't have been his predecessors. It had to be Taggart.

And now he himself was next in line for execution. How many assassins did Heward control, for Chrissake? Had Ryder been his successor? Would Heward now have to recruit someone new, or did he already have someone in place?

Greeve had smoked only two of the cigarettes Lisa had

bought for him in France the previous day. He lit one now.

Ryder had been supplied with photographs of both himself and Lisa. Therefore she was a target. Her fears were not exaggerated. But surely there was no way she could be an official target. That just didn't make sense. Therefore it was a private hit. Therefore....

Therefore Heward had to be selling his assassins' services on the open market!

Greeve went to the mini-bar and opened a quarter bottle of cognac and added a splash of soda to the glass. He drank as he paced up and down the room.

It was coming together. It was making sense.

He stopped abruptly.

All the time he'd worked for Heward, all the years when he'd believed he was an honourable assassin, he had in fact been a murderer!

The glass snapped in his hand and he stared in surprise at the brandy dripping from his fingers and the sliver of glass protruding from his palm. The brandy stung the open wound.

It wasn't a bad cut. He cleaned up the mess and held his handkerchief pressed against his palm to stop the bleeding and poured another glass, not bothering with the soda.

He was a murderer.

A strong physical reaction. Racing heart, sweat on the brow, trembling hands. Anger. A terrible anger.

Twelve years of his life. Twelve years of a dirty and dangerous job. Twelve years of believing he was doing something useful for his country, something valuable, something *honourable*. No doubt some of the kills had been genuine: Playboy, for instance. Boetsen. Brady. Picard. All dangerous men, men who had been a threat to his country. But Hugo Castelle? Castelle must have been a private hit, killed for the same reason that Lisa had been targeted. Therefore Lisa was genuine. Bodo Roth? Hard to say. Lisa had been present when he'd excised Bodo Roth: had it been a set-up, a device to persuade him that Lisa was a genuine target? Heward knew his difficulty about killing women.

Fucking hell, one was enough! Just one illegal hit was enough to make him a murderer, a man who killed for money instead of the retained professional he had so naively imagined himself to be. He'd been manipulated, conned, deceived, cheated, *used*. Heward had made a fool of him.

He felt dirty, degraded, shabby. This must be what it felt like to be raped. It was almost a physical pain.

The glass was empty. He filled it again and drank and felt the strong spirit burning down his throat and setting his guts on fire and poured some more.

Cool it. Calm down. Take it easy.

Fuck that. He emptied the glass and refilled it.

Think. Stop and think. Use the brain. Use the wits God gave you.

He went to the bathroom and poured the brandy down the toilet. When he came back he took a sheet of the hotel stationery from the rack and began to consolidate his plans.

He was meeting Heward tomorrow. It would be easy to excise him, put one into the back of his head in the hotel room and walk away. But that would solve nothing: there was still the threat to Lisa. So long as she was in danger they were both in danger and they would have no peace.

He had no idea where Heward lived or worked. He almost certainly didn't even know Heward's real name. He knew where Carver kept his plane when he was in England, but not where he stayed. He had to put Heward and Carver in the same place at the same time before he could take action against them.

How?

He lit another cigarette and stared at the sheet of paper, trying to work it all out.

· Seventeen ·

They never met anywhere they might be seen together. That was one of the rules Lacey had made when he and Carver had first formed their association.

Fortunately, the American took a peasant's delight in the trappings of success and one of the ways he liked to spend his money was to have his meals brought to him in his suite. He liked the arrival of the waiter pushing the trolley, the spreading of the tablecloth, the laying out of the dishes, being poured a little of the wine for his approval, the eagerness with which the tip was accepted. No doubt he had seen it all in a movie; a James Bond movie, perhaps. Lacey despised Carver for his vulgarity.

Rossi opened the door and stood aside to let Lacey in. Carver was standing at the window, looking down at the street, wearing a ridiculous jacket with the Dallas Cowboys insignia sprawled garishly across the back. He turned and smiled without humour.

'Lacey, my friend. Tell me you are not the bearer of bad timings.'

'Some good news, some not so good news.'

'Go on. Tell me everything.'

Lacey glanced at the laden drinks trolley. He badly wanted a whisky.

'Give the man some courage, Rossi. He looks as if he needs it.'

There was an uncomfortable pause while the bodyguard methodically poured a large whisky and added an equal quantity of soda. Lacey remained standing in the middle of the room; it was unpleasantly reminiscent of being in the headmaster's study. *I am informed that you have been up to your nasty little tricks again, Lacey.* He took the glass offered by Rossi.

'In your own time, my friend.'

Lacey drank deeply. 'Lisa Castelle is dead. My man Ryder took care of that. Unfortunately, the man we knew as Alan Sinclair was in fact my best operative, John Greeve. He killed Ryder.'

Carver walked slowly across the room and stood over Lacey, his eyes narrowed, his mouth turned down at the corners. Lacey could smell his aftershave. Much too strong.

'Run that past me again, my friend.'

Lacey looked into his glass to avoid those penetrating eyes.

'I've been running John Greeve for the past twelve years. He's the man who carried out all the hits you requested, as well as the official ones. He is a superb hatchet man. What I did not know is that he had become involved with Lisa Castelle. He apparently saw her photograph and became infatuated with her and sought her out. He also saw her when he killed Bodo Roth, remember. His campaign to win the lady's affections was apparently successful, which is why they were together. He's been using the name Alan Sinclair and the description I was given didn't ring a bell.'

There was no need for Carver to know about the photograph of Greeve and Castelle supplied by Greasley.

'So you sent – Ryder, was it? – to kill Castelle and

Greeve. But Greeve was too good for Ryder.'

'Yes. It looks that way.'

'Careless, my friend. Incompetent, even.'

Lacey shook his head vigorously. 'Ryder was competent. I've used him twice before, on official hits, and he was reliable and efficient and discreet. He was to replace Greeve in due course.'

'He failed. He got killed.'

'Yes.'

'So this guy Greeve is running loose. How much does he know?'

'Nothing.'

'How do you know?'

'He called in. He wants a meet. He's badly cut up about Lisa Castelle, but he has no idea I'm responsible.'

'You hope.'

Lacey felt the first prickling of fear. 'He's distressed, angry, confused, but he trusts me. We don't like each other, but he trusts me.'

'You hope.'

'I'm sure....'

'No you're not! I can tell by your face. You're not sure at all. You don't know what he got out of Ryder before he killed him. You don't know what Lisa Castelle told him about me. You don't know what he's doing now. You don't know if he's looking for me right now with a gun in his hand. Maybe he's looking for you.'

Lacey swallowed the last of his whisky. 'I've already decided he should be excised. Just to be sure.'

'Now you're talking like a man who knows which side of the toast is buttered. This guy has to be wiped now. And I mean NOW!'

Lacey recoiled. Carver rarely raised his voice. When he did the effect was startling.

'It's in hand.'

'What do you mean, in hand?'

'Before I started running assassins, I did the job myself.'

'You were a professional killer?' Carver sounded derisive.

'Yes, I was.'

'How many?'

'Five.'

'How did you do it?'

'Two with a rifle, two with a pistol, one with a garrotte.'

Carver stared at him for a long time. 'I think you're telling me the truth, my friend.'

'Yes, I am.'

'Who'd've believed it, for Chrissake? You don't look like a professional hitman.'

Lacey sensed he was recovering a little of his authority. 'What do professional hitmen look like?'

Carver shrugged and flashed his teeth. 'Hell, I don't know. Like you, maybe. When are you going to do it? I mean, I do not want this guy running around with his head full of stuff which could do me harm. I want him put away NOW!'

'I'm meeting him tomorrow night.'

'Is he as good as you say he is?'

'He is very good. He was good before I recruited him and he got better. He's had plenty of practice.'

'Then you're going to need help.'

Lacey glanced at the impassive Rossi. 'I won't say no to that.'

Carver tapped Lacey in the chest with a thick finger. 'I mean me as well, my friend. I don't just sell guns: I use them.'

'Fine.' Lacey managed a smile. 'I won't turn down some help. Fine.'

'OK. Let's make plans.' Carver took Lacey's empty glass and held it out to Rossi. 'Sit down, my friend. We

have to come up with a plan which will leave your man
Greeve outnumbered and outgunned, in a place where no
one is going to hear the sound of gunfire. And we're
going to have to arrange all this in a way which does not
make your man suspicious. I take it he will be suspicious?'

Lacey nodded. 'His fancy woman has just been killed
and he's expecting another attempt on his own life. Yes,
he'll be on the alert.'

Carver dropped into an armchair; it creaked in protest
at his weight. He grinned suddenly.

'Hell, this takes me back! It's been a long time since I
blew someone away. I miss it. The best buzz there is! The
last time I killed a guy I fucked for twenty-four hours
non-stop. They were calling reinforcements from every
cathouse in Dallas. Now does it grab you, my friend?
Does it give you a high?'

Lacey thought of Angela, sour-faced at her dressing-
table, rubbing cream into her dry hands.

'I'm English.'

It was not a day for walking in the woods. The rain had
stopped but the grass was still wet and every movement
of the wind brought heavy drops of water down from the
trees. Greeve felt the damp creeping through his shoes.

He reached the top of the small hillock and the flat land
to the south opened out before him. He heard the rising
scream of aircraft engines and watched what looked like a
Jetstream 41 accelerate down the runway past the two big
hangars and the control tower and take off. It vanished
quickly into the overcast.

He opened the leather case and took out the 20x50
binoculars he had bought that morning and rested his
shoulder against a tree and adjusted the eyepiece and the
focus until both images showed the control tower clearly.
A man in a blue boilersuit appeared from a door and it

was almost possible to read the logo on his breast pocket.

Greeve swung the binoculars gently left, studying each of the aircraft parked on the hardstanding. Two Cessnas, a Bell Jetranger with its rotors spinning slowly, a brightly painted biplane. The doors of the first hangar were wide open and he could see the tail section of a plane he didn't recognize, but the registration was not that of Carver's Learjet. In the background another small jet was being overhauled. The number was not visible but he checked what he could see of it against the photograph in the advertisement in *Flight International* and concluded that it was not the plane he was trying to find.

The doors of the other hangar were only slightly open. He tried to peer through the narrow gap into the gloom but the shapes were too indistinct to be recognized.

It was almost two hours before a Land Rover drove up and parked and three men got out and opened the big doors and went in. By that time Greeve had studied the whole airfield minutely, watched various planes and helicopters come and go, and even passed an interesting hour observing the local wildlife.

Carver's plane was parked immediately inside the big door, on the left, its tail section with the registration number clearly visible. Carver was in England.

Greeve returned the glasses to their case and walked back to the car, relieved that it would not now be necessary to make the fake phone call to the airfield asking if the American's plane was there. That would have been dangerous. Word might have got back to Carver, alerting him to the possibility that something was going on, that someone was looking for him.

His case was in the boot. He changed into dry shoes and socks and drove north-east, heading for Colchester. When he arrived he booked in at the hotel under the name Heward had supplied, took his case up to his room and then went back out to explore the immediate surroundings, noting the position of the car-park and the fire escape and rear exit, the direction of the traffic flow, the proximity of the nearest traffic lights, anything which might be useful in a crisis.

Back in the room he checked his watch and calculated the time in New York. Lisa would still be at the magazine offices, researching. He showered and changed and went downstairs to the bar.

Heward walked in an hour later. Their eyes met through the glass door of the bar but they did nothing to acknowledge each other. Heward entered the bar ten minutes later and ordered a whisky and water and sat down at the next table and opened his *Times*. The pencilled numbers at the top left-hand corner of the front page were clearly visible. Room 23, 7 p.m. Half an hour to wait. Greeve rose and went to the bar and ordered another brandy.

Lacey read the Bernard Levin column without taking in any of the meaning.

Greeve was looking suntanned and lean and fit. And calm, which was a relief. He had half-expected the sergeant to be in a state of agitation. The working classes, in Lacey's opinion, had only a tenuous grip on their emotions. They didn't know how to behave. They didn't know how to contain their anger and nurse it secretly until the chance arose to exact a satisfying revenge.

Ten to seven. He left the bar and went up to his room and poured two whiskies from his flask. Greeve walked in at seven o'clock exactly, locking the door behind him. Heward switched on the television and turned up the sound.

'Sit down, Sergeant. Whisky there. I postponed this

meeting until I had something definite to tell you. What I'm about to say is top secret, but under the circumstances I think you need to know.'

Greeve slumped into the hard chair beside the window. Lacey sat down on the bed and put his glass on the bedside cabinet. He could feel the hard lump of the automatic pistol under the right-hand pillow. Was Greeve carrying? Nothing showed.

'From what I've learned yesterday and today, you were not a target, Sergeant. Lisa Castelle was. You just happened to be with her at the time. Was there any direct attempt to take you out?'

'Yes.'

'You're sure of that?'

'Yes.'

'That makes sense, I suppose. We're dealing here with a nasty organization. We have evidence that Miss Castelle was not their first victim.'

'Like her father, for instance.'

Greeve was being difficult. He seemed to be in one of his confrontational moods. Well, Lacey knew how to handle him.

'Hugo Castelle puzzled us for a long time. We contracted you to excise him because everything pointed to his being an Iraqi recruit. There's a possibility that we may have been wrong. The Cousins have released just enough hints to persuade us that he was playing a very deep game and that he did it so successfully that we were fooled into thinking he was genuine. I regret to have to say that you may have excised an innocent man. A brave man. No blame attaches to you, of course. It was our decision, our mistake. Incidentally, if Hugo Castelle was innocent, it would appear to follow that his daughter was innocent as well.'

'So who are these people who killed Lisa?'

'Carver Arms and Systems of Dallas. Which really means Eugene Carver. It's an outwardly legal company but it's actually a cover for the selling of all kinds of military equipment to people who can't buy on the open market. Carver seems to be able to lay his hands on some very high-tech stuff as well as the usual automatic weapons and ammunition and so on. It's difficult to be certain – we need the Cousins' help in this and we're not getting it – but it looks as if a lot of the material he sells is stolen. There's a possibility that he may even have supplied the Iraqis with some of the equipment they need to develop their nuclear capability.'

'Lisa mentioned Carver Arms. She was on to them. Do you actually have any proof that Ryder was working for them?'

Lacey took a sip from his glass and relaxed against the pillows. The fool was taking it all in.

'We've been keeping an eye on Carver when he visits London, which he does regularly. He was observed meeting a man about ten days ago, someone we hadn't seen before. We did a routine check. It was a man by the name of David Ryder. That meant nothing to us at the time, of course. We ran a quick check: ex-lieutenant, good family, big farm in Shropshire, no form. Maybe it was a chance meeting, maybe he was just looking for a job. There seemed to be nothing suspicious about the incident. In retrospect, the meeting takes on a much greater importance.'

'So Lisa was killed on the orders of Eugene Carver.'

'We've nothing that would stand up in court, but it looks that way.'

'And Carver visits this country regularly?'

'He's here now.'

Greeve seemed to tense in his chair.

'Where is he?'

'We don't know where he's staying this time – it's never the same place twice – but we know where he keeps his plane. He flies a Learjet, pilots it himself. I have some data here....'

Lacey took a photograph and a single sheet of typescript from his pocket.

'The photograph was published in a Dallas newspaper two years ago and is nothing special, but it might help. The description is rather sketchy because, of course, it doesn't include anything about his home address or what he drives or his habits: that wouldn't be relevant. I've requested any available information, but I have to say I don't have the clout necessary to persuade other sections to mount a full-scale operation. I've already pulled in all the debts owing to me and made promises I hope I won't have to keep. The best I can say is that Carver arrived yesterday morning and he never stays more than forty-eight hours.'

'Why?'

'Why what?'

'Why tell me all this?'

Lacey shrugged. 'I assumed you might be interested in finding the man.'

'You're not issuing a contract on him?'

'No. I have no orders to that effect.'

'But if I were to take a personal interest how would you react?'

'I wouldn't. It's nothing to do with me. Remember, I don't know you. I've never heard of you. But I do feel guilty about what has happened; perhaps if we'd been more alert, or if there had been better inter-departmental communication, the young lady would still be alive. Giving you this information, I suspect, is just me trying to ease my guilt by giving you the chance of revenge. As I say, it's nothing to do with me what happens next. But if you need equipment....'

An automatic pistol appeared like magic in Greeve's hand. It looked like one of the FN High-powers. Lacey did his best not to flinch. Greeve displayed the gun for a moment.

'I have my own, thanks.'

'Ammunition?'

'Enough.'

'You appreciate ...'

'I can't go to you for help under any circumstances.'

'Exactly.'

'Understood. So where does he keep his plane?'

Heward left the hotel an hour later. Greeve, watching from the bedroom window, saw him cross the car-park carrying his case, get into a Volvo and drive away. It was raining again, the sky overcast. It would be a dark night. He looked at his watch and calculated the time in New York and picked up the phone and dialled.

'Miss Castelle, please. Room 1314.'

'One moment, please.'

'Alan?'

'How did you know it was me?'

'I wanted it to be you. How are you?'

'Fine. You?'

'Tired. Finished here. I haven't learned much more than I did yesterday. What about you?'

Greeve hesitated. This might be the last time he spoke to her and there was a lot he wanted to say.

'I've seen Carver's plane. He's in this country now.'

'I'll fly back tomorrow.'

'All right. I'll see you at my hotel. Call me from the airport.'

'OK. Love you.'

'Love you.'

Greeve replaced the phone. Coward! But how could he

have said what needed to be said over the phone, over 3,000 miles? That would have been even more cowardly than saying nothing.

Maybe it wouldn't matter. Maybe he'd never get the chance to tell her he'd killed her father. It might be better that way. Telling her the truth might do his conscience some good, would put an end to her search, but it would screw her up completely. All her life she would remember loving her father's murderer, making love to the man who had shot her father through the head, and the effect would be terrible. She might never be able to trust another man, ever. He couldn't do that to her. She was a woman who needed to love and be loved.

She'd had some bad luck in her life and it looked as if meeting him was the worst luck of all.

Greeve took his case downstairs and went to the reception desk. He was sorry, but he would have to leave unexpectedly. Heward had already settled the bill. He paid for the phone call to New York and went out to his car. It was raining steadily and the sky was already half-dark.

He drove back along the road he had driven earlier in the day, towards the airfield. About half-way to his destination he stopped at a motorway service station and, in the darkened car-park, pulled a dark-blue roll-neck jersey over his shirt and replaced his tweed jacket with one of heavy black leather. When he went into the restaurant he ordered a light meal and settled down to wait.

· Eighteen ·

Lacey braked to a halt behind a row of vehicles in a corner of a pub car-park two miles from the airfield. He had covered the distance from Colchester in what had to be record time and there had been several awkward moments on the wet roads in the dark. He took the holdall from the back seat and locked the Volvo and looked around to see Carver standing beside the rented Vauxhall with his hand raised; he hurried over and got into the back seat and Rossi set the car in motion.

'Well, my friend? Did it work?'

'Perfectly. I gave him almost the whole truth so that whatever he already knew would tally. He took it all in. He's looking for you and I've told him the one place he'll be able to find you is at the plane and that you'll be leaving the country tomorrow. He'll be on his way by now. In fact, he may not be far behind me.'

'What's he carrying?'

'FN High-power.'

'We can cope with that.' The gas Zippo flared and the smell of cigar smoke filled the car. 'What sort of mood is he in?'

'Determined. Cold. Unforgiving. He's angry but keeping it under control.'

'A dangerous man. Does he know about Rossi?'

'No.'

'So he'll be expecting to find me and no one else. Good. We'll go with the plan.'

A few minutes later Rossi stopped the car at the yellow metal gate; he got out and Carver and Lacey watched as the bodyguard stood in the glare of the headlights to release the padlock, the rain making dark spots on the back of his blue suit. He pushed the gate open and returned to drive through the opening then went back to relock the gate. Neither Carver nor Lacey made any move to assist. Rossi raced the car through the puddles on the hardstanding, the water drumming on the underside, and parked beside one of the hangars. They all got out and Rossi unlocked the small door set into the big sliding door and went through carrying a lighted torch; a few seconds later the overhead lights came on and Carver and Lacey followed. Rossi experimented with the array of switches until only three lights remained, illuminating a long workbench at the far left corner of the echoing space. The glow did not extend to the whole area, leaving the planes ghostly silhouettes in the gloom. The cold air carried the smell of aviation fuel and oil and paint.

They said nothing to each other. Rossi marched the length of the hangar, hung his jacket on a hook and struggled into an orange boilersuit too small for his barrel chest. Carver went to the Learjet and mounted the steps and vanished inside, to reappear carrying an odd-looking pump-action shotgun with a pistol grip.

Lacey looked at it with interest. 'What is it?'

'This is the Winchester Defender, my friend. Twelve-gauge, seven rounds, eighteen-inch barrel. A terrifying weapon, very popular with the police and the FBI in the good old democratic US of A. Guaranteed to make any perpetrator change his mind about a shoot-out.' He began loading shells into the tubular magazine under the barrel.

'Are you going with your Heckler and Koch?'

'It's my favourite handgun. What does Rossi carry?'

'He's a traditionalist. He uses a Colt M1911A1.'

'It must be fifty years old.'

'It is, but it's in perfect condition. We see to that in the workshop. And he's deadly with it, and very fast. Trust him.'

'I do.' Lacey opened his holdall and took out a pair of waxed cotton trousers and pulled them on over his slacks. He zipped up the Barbour jacket and donned a dark-blue ski mask which left only his eyes and mouth showing. He fitted thin leather gloves over his hands, loaded the pistol and dropped it into his pocket.

'I'll get into position.'

'No shooting outside.'

'I know.'

'Good luck, my friend.'

'You too.'

Lacey walked across to the small door and out into the darkness. Odd, he thought; for a moment there we were almost friends. A touch of genuine shared emotion. It would blow over.

He moved to his left to where he was well away from the dim glow of light from the door then jogged across the hardstanding until he felt wet grass under his feet. He carried on for another twenty yards, stopping just short of the runway, then turned and looked back. The night was almost impenetrably black, the lit doorway seeming to hang suspended in space. The rain was still falling steadily; in the silence he could hear it hissing gently on the ground. He could just identify the roof of the hangar against the darkness of the sky.

He knelt on the grass and lay down carefully on his belly, using his elbows to take the weight, keeping his gloves dry, then pulled up the snap-on hood to protect his head. The pistol could stay in his pocket for the time being. In the darkness, prone like this, he was invisible.

How long till Greeve arrived? Not long, surely. The man was a professional, a planner, a thinker. He would want to get to know the territory before the action started. He was probably working on the assumption that Carver would fly out in the morning and would want to be in position before the American arrived. When they discussed the plan in Carver's suite it had been Lacey's opinion that Greeve would try to place himself inside the Learjet and wait there for Carver to show. That, Lacey had said, was what he would have done in the same situation. Carver and Rossi had agreed. It was noticeable that the two Americans had been prepared to take advice from the retired professional assassin. It had been good to see the respect in their eyes.

The cold from the ground was beginning to seep through to his skin, but the waxed cotton would keep him dry. He rested his chin on his crossed arms and watched the rectangle of light from under the protection of the hood.

Greeve left the service station a little after ten and continued his journey, keeping the speed down to a safe limit. When the signs appeared indicating that the airfield was a few miles ahead he visualized the road map he had studied that afternoon and turned off on to a side road and followed it until the church and cemetery appeared on his left. The turning he wanted was a few hundred yards further on. The lane was narrow, running between fields with an occasional farm entrance. A strange paradox, one he'd noticed many times before: the assassin moving unobserved in the midst of peaceful and unsuspecting daily life.

The road forked; he went left and bumped along a track

into a small stand of trees and switched off the lights and the engine. Total darkness; rain on the roof. He climbed out and zipped up the leather jacket and turned up the collar and stood there for five minutes, letting his eyes grow accustomed to the darkness, gradually managing to discern the difference between ground and sky. There were a number of distant lights showing in the surrounding countryside, but only one of them could be coming from the airport buildings, a single rectangle of faint yellow about 400 yards away. He used the binoculars and nodded with satisfaction and put the glasses back in the car and locked the door.

He stumbled across the verge to the low fence surrounding the airfield and stepped over into long wet grass and began to walk slowly towards the light, the rain soaking his hair and pattering gently on the leather of his jacket.

Rossi had set up a length of aluminium tubing in a vice and was idly pushing a file across it; the sound was distinct and would carry in the echoing space of the hangar. From the door he would look like a mechanic doing some rush job. He didn't like standing with his back to the danger, but he would do what the boss ordered, even if it was that little fart Lacey who had dreamed up the stakeout.

The Colt lay by his right hand, under a clean rag, loaded, the safety off, ready for instant action. He hoped he would get the chance to use it. In all his years of working for Gene Carver he had never been given the chance to use the gun for real. Before that, yes, back in the days when he ran with the gang in Miami; two kills and a possible, one of them a cop. He was respectable now, better paid and seeing the world, but he missed the excitement. Still, he'd promised Carla and he'd kept his promise and they had a nice house now, the cottage in the grounds of the boss's property, and the kids called Carver Uncle Gene, which he liked. He always gave them something special at Christmas and birthdays.

It would be good to drop this guy Greeve, the professional hitman, and see the boss's look of gratitude.

Greeve crossed the runway and then the strip of grass between the runway and the hardstanding outside the hangar. His feet were soaked through, his trouser-legs wet to the knees. He kept his hands in the pockets of the leather jacket to keep them dry and warm, the butt of the High-power held loosely in one hand, the spare magazine in the other.

When he reached the edge of the hardstanding he stopped and crouched on one knee and blanked off the lit doorway with one hand while he tried to identify any dangers, but he could see nothing. When he studied the airfield from the hillock earlier in the day he had noted that the aluminium sides of the hangars were painted a light tan colour; now, in the darkness, they were invisible even from about fifty yards.

He rose and walked across the tarmac, keeping well to the left of the doorway. When he reached the building he sighted along it towards the door but saw nothing between himself and the tiny spread of light. He moved silently towards the doorway, his fingers trailing along the metal, looking for the division in the sliding doors. When he found it he tried to see through the gap but there was a rebate which blanked off the opening.

He moved on and reached the small open door and stopped before the light touched his body and listened intently. A regular squeaking sound, coming from a distance, setting his teeth on edge. What the hell was it?

* * *

Carver sat on one of the passenger seats in the darkness of the Learjet, the Defender across his knees, uncomfortable in the dark-blue flak jacket. The door of the plane was open and he had a clear view of the dusty concrete immediately in front of the small door they had left open. A semi-circle of wet had developed from the rain blowing in from outside. The screech of Rossi's filing was irritating but essential. The man was totally loyal but sometimes annoyingly subservient: give him an order and he carried it out and went on carrying it out until he was told to stop.

Poor bloody Lacey, out there in the darkness, lying on his little pot belly on the wet grass! Carver grinned at the thought. The Englishman was so damn *fragile*. His pride was fragile, his authority was fragile, his confidence was fragile. Even his sexuality was fragile. What sort of relationship did he have with his wife? He never spoke of her, but the embarrassed eagerness with which he grabbed the chance of a quick screw suggested he wasn't getting what he needed at home.

Lacey's main virtue, Carver had long since decided, was his greed. The Englishman had sold information directly damaging to his country, many times; he had betrayed his fumbling organization without hesitation; he had sent his hitmen out to kill people who were not enemies of his country. And all for the money. Tonight they were about to kill a man who had worked loyally for Lacey for twelve years but there had been no hint of remorse in the pale-blue eyes.

All of which made Lacey a valuable employee, well worth the money Carver paid him. Money, in Carver's opinion, was the great motivator. Money let you take care of all the other motivations, the other needs: the women and the plane and the cars and the hotel suites and the permanent bodyguard and the clothes and the house and the gun collection and all the other things that showed the world just how successfully Eugene Carver had risen from the trash to the top of the heap.

He shifted slightly in the seat and wiped the palms of his hands on his trousers.

First they had to get Greeve to talk; they had to find out just how much Lisa Castelle had uncovered about Carver Arms, find out if the bitch had put anything on paper and hidden it away. But Greeve would not want to talk. Carver had said nothing about this to Lacey, but in his view the essential preliminary had to be severe shock and pain, like having a leg blown away by a blast from the 12-gauge.

Greeve moved out from the building, into the darkness, until he reached a point where the glimmer of light from the doorway would not illuminate him. He moved slowly to his right, seeing the first of the parked planes and the deep shadows inside the hangar. He kept moving until he could identify the source of the light, a row of three overhead lamps above a bench at which a man in an orange boilersuit was working, filing away at something clamped in a vice. The whole scene looked almost ridiculously normal and void of threat.

Was the man Carver? Greeve stared hard at him, running through the checklist Heward had provided, visualizing the photograph. Broad-backed, certainly, but not tall enough, and the hair was short, a crewcut, not the thick wavy rug the American favoured. And definitely too young. It couldn't be Carver.

Greeve kept moving until he had traversed the whole doorway and was looking at the dim outline of Carver's Learjet, parked just inside the hangar on the left, its door open, the steps down. There seemed to be no one else in the hangar. The sound of filing continued, slow and repetitive and painful to the ears.

There was nothing to be gained by remaining out here in the rain and the cold. Greeve moved up to the door, took the High-power from his pocket and slipped the safety catch, paused for a moment in the deep darkness outwith the cone of light, then moved quickly and silently inside and immediately went to his right, into the shadow behind a parked plane. Looking back, he saw that he had left wet footprints on the concrete of the floor, but there was nothing he could do about that.

He crouched under a wing and searched the hangar at ground level for any sign of legs, anyone hidden, anyone waiting for him. Nothing. He tried to listen beyond the scrape of file on metal, trying to catch any hint of any other sound. Nothing.

Lacey had watched Greeve's antics at the door, a tiny smile at the corner of his mouth. He saw the silhouetted body move slowly across the spread of light, far enough back from the door to be invisible to anyone inside the hangar, and had then seen him take out the pistol and pass through the doorway and vanish. Had Carver seen him? Definitely, unless the fat peasant had fallen asleep, which seemed unlikely.

Lacey rose and shook the worst of the water off the waxed cotton and took out the Heckler and Koch and moved the safety catch.

God, but this took him back! He could feel the cold excitement, the hurried pulse, the tingling nerve ends. He felt strong and quick and alert.

Maybe he'd experiment with Carver's theory that a kill created a sexual high. Even allowing for Texan exaggeration there had to be something in the idea. It would be different with one of the coloured girls at Mrs

Norman's. Different from Angela. Maybe two girls.

He walked slowly towards the door, the automatic hanging by his side, finger resting on the trigger guard, ears alert for any sound from inside the building.

Carver had seen Greeve enter the building, but the assassin's arrival had been much sooner than they had expected and he had vanished into the shadows too quickly for him to raise the Defender and get off a shot. Had Rossi heard him? The sound of filing continued without interruption.

What now? Wait. Take it easy. The sudden kick in his pulse rate was good. This was Greeve, the expert hatchet man, fourteen or fifteen kills to his credit, a dangerous man; but he was outnumbered, out-thought, surrounded. Lacey would have seen him enter and would be closing in right now. In a moment he would be outside the door, gun in hand, invisible in the darkness with Greeve caught between him and the lights.

Wait.

Greeve watched the man at the bench for a while, waiting for some kind of change, a glance backwards, a pause, anything at all. Nothing happened. The man kept on filing away at whatever he was filing, slowly, rhythmically, the rasp of the file on the metal raucous in the cold air.

Time to move.

Carver watched the shadow under the Cessna, his eyes narrowed in an unconscious attempt to penetrate the blackness. The Winchester Defender sat comfortably in his big hands.

Show yourself, asshole. Give me a hint. Just a blink of movement is all I need.

Greeve moved silently out of the shadow, his body crouched, the FN High-power held in the approved two-handed grip. He was heading for the shadow behind the Bell Jetranger.

Carver brought up the Defender and aimed at Greeve's legs and fired and pumped and fired again and again for a third time. The explosions were stunning in the confines of the plane.

Greeve sensed the flash a fraction of a second before the pellets hit. The sound came next, then the pain, but by that time he was moving, two long strides and a dive into the blackness below the helicopter. The second and third shots exploded off the concrete behind him and crashed into the aluminium wall of the hanger.

Hit, but not badly. Bleeding, but not life-threatening.

The man at the bench was moving, reaching for something under a rag. A gun, definitely.

The shotgun was more dangerous. Three shots, therefore a pump action. Two more, maybe four more, depending on the model. He snatched a glance at the Learjet: he had moved out of sight of anyone inside the plane.

The man in the orange boiler suit was turning and dropping into a crouch, very fast, a Colt .45 in his hands. Greeve steadied and double-tapped just as the man fired. The .45 slug hit the helicopter's inflation bag beside Greeve's head and passed through it and whined momentarily off the metal skid into the underside of the fuselage. The man slid down into a sitting position, the Colt falling from his hand and clattering on the floor.

'Lacey! Lacey! He's under the chopper!'

Lacey. So that was Heward's real name. Unless he'd given Carver a false name as well.

The shotgun appeared at the door of the Learjet and

fired once, the flame bright in the darkness, but Carver hadn't risked putting his head out to take aim and the pellets went wide.

'I've got him pinned down under the chopper! Get him!'

'I see him!'

'Hit him!'

Two shots from an automatic pistol in the doorway, then two more.

'Got him!'

'You sure?'

'Absolutely!'

Carver climbed down the steps from the plane, the shotgun held at the ready, and walked across the concrete towards the helicopter. The man in the doorway raised his pistol and shot him twice through the head. The big body went down like a puppet with the strings cut.

Greeve crawled out from under the Jetranger and pulled himself to his feet.

'Hurt?' Ryder pulled off the ski mask. Lacey's Barbour jacket and trousers were too small for him.

Greeve felt his legs. 'Maybe a dozen pellets. Bloody sore, but no major damage. I'll need surgery, but it should be possible to pass it off as a shooting accident. Lacey?'

'Broken neck, poor chap.'

'What did you shoot at?'

'That tyre over there.'

'Any difficulties?'

Ryder made the Heckler and Koch safe and dropped it into his pocket. 'I was in position just half an hour before they arrived. I know your call gave me plenty of time, but I had trouble finding the place in the dark. I saw them arrive, then one of them come back out and I recognized him as Jackson. At least, the man I knew as Jackson.'

'Lacey. I knew him as Heward.'

'Uh-huh. He did exactly what I'd have done: went out about seventy yards and lay down. He vanished. I got close, but it wasn't until you arrived and came inside that he got up and I was able to take him out.'

Greeve hobbled over to Carver and looked down at him.

'Check the one over there by the bench.'

Ryder walked over. 'He's dead. Two in the centre of the chest, less than an inch apart. You're very good.'

'Thank you. You're not bad yourself.'

'All this skill and we're now both out of work. Do you think we might....'

'I'm retiring. I have retired.'

'Oh, well. I suppose I can always go back to running the family farm. How about you?'

'I have some savings. See if there's a first-aid kit in the Lear.'

'Sorry. Should have thought of that.' Ryder climbed into the plane. A light came on. A minute later he leaned out of the opening and beckoned. 'Come on up. There's everything we need here.'

Greeve struggled up the steps and collapsed into a seat.

'Very fancy. No expense spared.'

Ryder opened the green plastic box and pulled on a pair of surgical gloves.

'Pull up your trouser-legs. Christ! Nasty.'

'I think it looks worse than it really is.'

'Elevate your legs. It reduces the bleeding.'

While Ryder worked, Greeve looked around. There was a black leather pilot's case on the seat across the aisle. He hefted it over, grunting at the weight, and opened it.

'I don't think we need worry too much about our financial futures.'

Ryder paused in the act of applying the wound dressing and looked into the case.

'Bloody hell! These are thousand-dollar bills!'

'And lots of them. Fifty-fifty seems appropriate.'

'Very appropriate. I'm very glad I didn't manage to excise you, John.'

'So am I.'

Ryder tied off the last dressing. 'I'll run you to a hospital. Is that where we'll part forever?'

'Not quite. I need you to appear at a hotel in Haringey tomorrow. Lisa thinks I killed you. It's putting a bit of a strain on our relationship.'

'No problem.'

'Right, my friend, let's go.'

'Lean on me.'

They paused at the hangar door and looked back at the two bodies lying on the cold concrete.

'I thought I was an honourable assassin,' Greeve said bitterly. 'I really thought I could take some pride in my work.'

'I know. I felt the same.'

Greeve shrugged. 'Screw them all. I've only one regret.'

'What's that?'

'That you got the chance to hit Lacey. I wanted to do that.'

'He's still dead.'

'There's that. Let's go.'

Newport Libraries

THIS ITEM SHOULD BE RETURNED OR
RENEWED BY THE LAST DATE
STAMPED BELOW.

Your co-operation is requested in returning this item to the
library from which it was issued.   3/2